Mukta Sathe is a young lawyer who has worked in Mumbai and Pune. She has written several articles for law journals. This is her first novel. She is interested in travel, constitutional law, literature and sports, as well as being a cat lover. She lives in her hometown, Pune.

A
Patchwork
Family

Mukta Sathe

SPEAKING
TIGER

SPEAKING TIGER PUBLISHING PVT. LTD
4381/4, Ansari Road, Daryaganj
New Delhi 110002

First published in paperback by Speaking Tiger 2018

ISBN: 978-93-88326-84-1
e-ISBN: 978-93-88070-24-9

10 9 8 7 6 5 4 3 2 1

Typeset in Arno Pro by by SÜRYA, New Delhi

Printed in India by Nutech Print Services - India

For my parents,
Dr. Dhanmanjiri Sathe and Mr. Makarand Sathe,
for being my source of inspiration and strength.

AJOBA

1

SHE HAS JUST CALLED TO TELL ME SHE IS IN A TAXI ON HER way to Pune, where I live, from Mumbai, which is now her home. She will reach in four-and-a-half hours, hopefully. If she reaches any sooner it will mean that she—or rather, the taxi driver—has been driving far too fast on the ghats. But maybe that really does not hold true now. An eighty-five-year-old man like me, who has driven an Ambassador all my life, may consider that the right amount of time, but today the cars are much better and the roads are much better too. And this generation is different. They want everything quicker. They are in a hurry and they don't want to wait. They're running, always. So if my friend comes earlier, I must not get angry at her.

I call her my friend, but she is my granddaughter's age. Her grandfather was my dearest friend, and she has always called me Ajoba as well. If I call her my friend now, it's because she has been forced to grow up so much in the last couple of years that it is impossible for me to look at her as a child. And it is also true that she is twenty-nine years old. Not really a child at all.

I live alone in my house in Pune. My wife passed away a little less than ten years ago, from cancer. My two sons live in the US with their families. When they came back to say their final goodbyes to their mother, my sons asked me to move to the US with them. But I declined their offer. I've spent my entire life here and, at seventy-five, I was fit enough to live alone. They were worried at first and used to call me every day, speak with me for hours. They still call me once a week and come to meet me every year with my grandchildren and daughters-in-law.

At the age of seventy-five it was easy enough for me to live alone. But now, ten years have passed and it's not that easy. But it's even more difficult for me to go to America now. And even if I went, what would I do there? So, when my friend invited me to come and live with her in Mumbai, I accepted the offer at once.

She lives alone in a two-bedroom flat in Navi Mumbai which she bought recently, and commutes for three hours every day, using a local train to go to her office. She works in a law firm as a lawyer. Even now that I am going to live with her, I don't think I'll see her much. I guess I'll 'meet' her only on Sundays. That's sad, but not unheard of in modern households. However, an old man like me, living with a young woman, without any blood relationship or romantic relationship between us—that's not common. At least, I have never heard of an arrangement like this. But seeing that both of us don't have any real family left, I think that this patchwork family might work. We will have to make do with it anyway.

She had come last Sunday, too, to transfer some of my possessions to her house. I have put all my books, my clothes, a few ornaments and, most importantly, photographs into cardboard boxes. My pillows, bed sheets, utensils and other small items are also all packed and ready to be moved. My bigger furniture, including my TV, will stay here. But I have taken my transistor, tape recorder and cassettes. When she saw my old and battered tape recorder, she gave me an understanding smile and at that moment I knew that I had become very old indeed.

I am renting out my flat and have already signed an agreement with the tenants. She looked into all the legal aspects. She was also very quick to remind me that I had never quite approved of her entering a profession which I found both despicable and intimidating.

Last Sunday, she took away most of the boxes and now she is coming to fetch me! The month of May is half over and it is comforting to know that I will have enough time to shift and to settle down in Mumbai before the onset of the monsoons in June. It rains very heavily in Mumbai every year, but this time, because of climate change, scientists are predicting an 'unpredictable' change in weather. Let's see how much rain we are to receive in 2014.

It took me more than two months to pack all my boxes. First, I had to go and buy the boxes. Getting out of the house requires lot of planning and energy at my age. And then, I had to go to the shop three times, because the tradition in our city prevents our shopkeepers from giving us everything that we want in one visit. Thus, after a week, I had finally assembled all that I required. Then began the tedious process of packing. I had to empty all my cupboards and classify all my possessions. In the process, I managed to clear most of my house of the dust that had settled, layer upon layer, on all the surfaces, a chore which my housekeeper had most conveniently omitted to perform. Then I had to decide what to keep and what to throw away, a process even more painful than dusting, for, at my age, one wants to cling on to every photo, every shirt, every newspaper clipping and indeed, every memory. In the end, I discovered that I had decided to keep most of my things.

But I gave away my typewriter. I had hardly ever used it. There are many things which I had acquired with great enthusiasm, either because they were new scientific inventions in those times, or because I had seen them in movies (the typewriter belonging to the latter category). I had hardly ever used them. These included a vacuum cleaner (which is not of much use in Pune), an electronic razor (which I never used as I found the whole idea absurd) and most recently, an electronic cigarette (even though I do not smoke and seventy-five was a bit too old to begin). I had given away all the other things some time after my wife's death, but the typewriter had remained. My wife had loved it, and I had kept it to honour her memory. She liked typing on it and she liked polishing it even more. When my eldest son first went to the US, she had typed a letter on it and posted it to him. I can still remember the look of delight on her face when she finally posted that letter. My son still has it. He brought it with him last year when he came to visit me. My grandchildren did not believe me when I told them that I still possess a typewriter. When they met me after their long journey from New Jersey to Pune, even before drinking water, the first thing they asked me was to verify their father's statement about the typewriter. When I assured them that I really had one, they demanded that I should produce it. The look on their faces when they saw the old neglected typewriter was very similar to the one on my wife's when she'd sent that letter. They found it 'very cool'. They cleaned it, polished it and played with it. They considered it an antique, to be kept in a museum. I sold it as trash.

After deciding what to throw away and what to keep, I sorted the remainder into groups and started to fill up the boxes and label them. I had left some clothes out; everything else in went into the boxes. Then she came last Sunday and took away as many boxes as she could fit into the taxi. Only two boxes remain, which she will take today, along with me. I shouldn't have sold that typewriter. It would have just required one more box.

Anyway, she will come today and the process that started three months ago, of me moving into her house, will end. But it is still a long time till I can actually rest. That will only happen after the two months which I have given myself to unpack. She will not understand this. She did not understand why it took me so long to pack in the first place. When she had shifted to Mumbai three years ago, she had hardly taken two days to pack. But she had even fewer possessions than I do and more importantly, a far, far fitter body.

The pain begins with the right big toe, and then my right leg begins to shake, violently. In a few hours the pain spreads upwards, up to my right hip and the right side of my waist. It's like a blade of ice cutting through all my muscles at the same time. I take painkillers. Sometimes they help, sometimes they don't. At my age, even medicines seem to have a mind of their own and their decisions are usually unfavourable to me. Then the back pain begins near the middle of my spine and all I can do is lie down. I keep flipping from side to side when my body hurts from being in one position for too long, and when I get too tired to do even that, I just lie in one position muttering under my breath, cursing the pain and pleading with it, all at once. Then I get too tired to do that as well. But I pull through every time. I don't know how, but I do. So when it took me three months to pack I did not find it alarming. I had done things very quickly, I thought. Lifting things up made my back worse for some days, but my mood was much better. I had something to look forward to. Something much more interesting than the daily serials which I watch on TV or the cricket matches or even the football World Cup, which is going to be held in Brazil this year. From tomorrow, I will not have anything to look forward to. But settling in will take some time…

Even though she shouldn't take less than four and a half hours to reach, I cannot help glancing at my watch every couple of minutes. I am worried that the driver will drive too fast, but at the same time I also know that I will be worried if she is late. But now I am going to live with her. What if she gets late coming home one day? I will call her then. Better still, I will ask her to install that software on her mobile through which I will be able to track her. But will she accept this request, or will she get angry if I ask her to install it? I don't know.

I will ask her anyway. I am too old to take this tension now. I think she will understand why I get so worried and she will forgive me. You would understand the extent of my apprehension only if you knew the past. How this patchwork

family came into being is a long story. And that is what I am
going to tell you here.

When she invited me to come and live with her, I was
quite surprised. But I was in need of other humans to talk
to, in need of a family—and thus, I accepted immediately.
Today, when I leave this house, I know that I'll probably
never come back. Travelling is not very easy at my age. But
I have no regrets. I already consider her my family. And I
need her because of my age. A comforting voice. Someone
who will notice if I die.

Till last Sunday I failed to understand why she would
want me to live with her. She rings me up regularly, but can
come to meet me only once in six months. When I opened the
door and received her last Sunday, she greeted me with her
customary smile and 'Hi Ajoba'. A flood of memories came
to my heart. It gave me such happiness. But that happiness
lasted only a few minutes. I looked at her this time and I
actually saw her. She has changed. I compared the woman
she is to the child that I had once been acquainted with.
The smile on her face didn't suit her. Her eyes have changed
too. As a child, her eyes used to be vibrant, but today, that
enthusiasm has been replaced by determination. Already, at
the age of twenty-nine, she is determined.

And I understood why she called me—because she needs
me, too. I need somebody younger and she needs somebody
older. We both need a family. And I am as close to a family
as she can get. Of course, she can marry and have children.
But she no longer has her 'family of birth'. Inviting me to live
with her is as close as she can come to that.

Leo Tolstoy writes in *Anna Karenina*: 'All happy families resemble one another; every unhappy family is unhappy in its own way.' True, very true. The history of how her family was destroyed is very traumatic. And the reasons that can lead to the destruction of a family can be even more varied. Even when most of the members of the family are still alive. But they, her relatives, have ceased to be a family. Nor are they a part of any new family. They are just individuals.

So we both try to build a patchwork family.

2

I still remember a Sunday nine years ago. It was a hot summer morning, somewhere in the middle of April 2005. I was sitting in my dear friend Shridhar's house, reading a newspaper and relaxing under the fan. This had become my routine on Sundays, ever since I had lost my wife about six months earlier. Shridhar Natu and I had been friends from childhood and he, too, had lost his wife a year before. Spending time together provided some comfort. On weekdays, we used to meet in a small park at seven every morning. Near the centre of the city and very close to both our houses, it was the ideal place for a morning walk together. We used to walk for about half an hour and then sit and chat. And we used to have so many things to tell each other. Then, almost every day, he would come over to my house for breakfast. I had employed a cook and we could eat in peace. It was better, he said, than having breakfast at his own house where all the other members of the family rushed around.

His family accepted this routine, which was altered only on Sundays. On Sunday everybody had their weekly day off, and they convinced him that it was much better to have me over for breakfast instead. His family had accepted my presence very cordially. Most of them had known me for their entire lives. The term 'family friend' is under threat today, but it is the truest description of my relationship with them. By their friendly acceptance of what could have been viewed as a rather unwelcome intrusion into their private time together as a family, they ensured that I did not feel lonely. They gracefully offered me a distraction from my pain, ignoring the inconvenience that it cost them.

Thus, that Sunday, I was sitting in a chair in my friend's living room. The building was built on a slope so that one side was closer to the ground. The house being on the first floor, Shridhar's children and grandchildren often considered it more practical to enter from the balconies attached to all three bedrooms and the living room, to the utter dismay of their parents. They were so close to the ground that it was easy for a young child to climb in or go out.

To the left of the door was what can be called the dining area. There was no wall or partition between the two rooms. A wooden dining table, encircled by six wooden chairs was placed in this space. Behind the dining area was the kitchen, again, with no walls or partitions. The three parts were one L-shaped room with no barriers to vision or sound between them.

Luckily for us, the living-room balcony faced west, protecting us from the scorching heat of the April morning sun. From where I was sitting, I could see the balcony on my right as well as what was going on in the dining area and the kitchen on my left. My friend was sitting in his armchair with his back to the balcony. This was his fixed spot. If anyone else sat on his armchair he disliked it immensely, but he did not make that person get up. He merely muttered under his breath till the person got up of his or her own accord. And then he used to always say that he had not made anyone get up! He was a true democrat, he often claimed. 'How can I not be? I heard Pandit Nehru's "Tryst with Destiny" speech at midnight on the fifteenth of August, 1947,' he would say with an expression of great pride, either innocently failing to acknowledge or deliberately choosing to ignore the looks of exasperation on the faces of all others present. He also, unfortunately, never failed to mention that he had volunteered to join the Quit India movement. But he selectively omitted that he had not actually participated in the movement because he'd been considered too young.

But that day, nobody else was occupying his seat and we were thus saved the entire drama. When I looked at him, I remembered my childhood, a great portion of which I had spent in his company. He had changed physically of course, but was fundamentally still very much the same. I like to remember him as the skinny boy in an off-white shirt and brown shorts who would race me to school barefoot. But he had also aged like me. At seventy-five he still had remarkably thick hair. His hair, like him, had a mind of its own and refused to take the shape he wanted. Despite a wide range of hair oils and much coaxing, his hair simply pointed up at the sky, towards the God in whom he firmly believed. His dark-brown eyes could be seen from behind the round spectacles which he perched on his long and slightly crooked nose. He was reading a Marathi newspaper intently, leaning forward with his brow furrowed in concentration. The fingers of his left hand would be placed momentarily on his Adam's apple and then moved up through his grey beard, up to his chin. He had a habit of repeating this action when he was upset, which I found most irritating.

'Bloody Pakis,' he said.

The reasons why those two words may be muttered by a middle-class, urban, Brahmin Indian are so numerous that it was impossible for me to guess what he'd read about. Varied as the reasons may be, each is adequate to enrage people like him to an alarming degree. Even losing a cricket match is considered an occasion for mourning. So I did not inquire. Then, after a couple of moments, he turned to the sports page and relaxed, as did I.

'Doctor, do you want tea?' he asked. I assented and he got up to make it himself. He could not cook, but he loved to make tea for others. He also liked asking them if they had liked the tea. One day, some weeks after this Sunday morning, I would tell him that tea is only tea. Thereafter he would stop offering to make it for me. But that day he offered me the tea, and, at the same time also continued another very irritating habit of his—that of calling me 'Doctor'. He knew my first name very well. Indeed, we had grown up in the same chawl and, as I have mentioned, had been very good friends from childhood. He was a general surgeon; I a dentist. He thought that he therefore had the right to make fun of me and my pleasure in being called 'Doctor' by my patients. But I chose to ignore him, believing that he would weary of the joke, and resume calling me by my first name (my 'maiden name', my wife used to call it, implying that I had married my profession). But being an excellent example of Puneri stubbornness, he never gave up this habit.

His family consisted of his son, daughter-in-law and two grandchildren. I distinctly remember his son, Partha, being born, especially as my second son was born only a few months afterwards. I also remember that his wife had confided in me before her delivery, that as she unfortunately had only two daughters, she was praying this time she would have a son. She admitted to me rather shyly that she wanted her son to look like her husband, but to have a personality like mine. I had been glad to know that she held me in such high esteem, but I would have been happier if this regard had been extended to her daughters as well.

His wife's wish was fulfilled and their third child was a boy. But Partha left his mother's wishes unfulfilled: I have not met a person more different from me. He is an engineer and at that time—nine years ago—worked in a German multinational company in Pune. His elder sisters, Sunita and Asha, lived with their families in Mumbai, as they do still.

A few minutes after Shridhar returned with two mugs of steaming hot tea—impossible to drink in the heat—and made himself comfortable in his armchair, Partha came out from his bedroom and sat down. He was speaking rather animatedly on his cell phone with someone from his team in the office. After a few minutes, he started pacing up and down the room, apparently exasperated about something. He was frowning, his thick black eyebrows touching each other and giving him the expression of an angry cat. A graying tom cat, for at that time Partha was about fifty years old. He stopped pacing and started telling the person what was to be done, in brief, clipped sentences. After he had finished, he switched off the phone and went into the kitchen to drink a glass of water.

In the kitchen, his wife Anita was starting to cook

breakfast and lunch. She was five years younger than her husband, a slim, health-conscious woman with long, wavy hair which she tied up loosely. That day, she was wearing an apron over her sari, and had a tired look on her long oval face, her eyes looking smaller than ever as she frowned. The cook had not come and Anita's weekend was ruined. She had taught science in a school earlier, but had stopped after the birth of her first child, Janaki. When her younger child, Rahul, grew up a little, she resumed teaching, but instead of joining a school, she preferred to take tuitions in her home. Her classes for ninth- and tenth-standard students had become popular over the years, so it was only on Sundays that she had any time to rest. But today, when she wanted her the most, the cook had not come. Thus, after waiting till ten o'clock, Anita resigned herself to the cook's absence, and started cooking herself.

I have never had to cook myself. When I was young, my mother cooked for me, and when I grew older, my wife cooked. After my wife's death, I employed a cook. If my cook doesn't show up, there's always Domino's pizza! But I have always liked the sound of masala being added to boiling oil. I think if I had told Anita this at the time, she would have wanted to hit me! He who doesn't have to work has the leisure to find music in kitchen noises.

In the meantime, my friend's grandson, Rahul, came out of his room facing the kitchen. He wanted breakfast. His mother told him to sit with us in the living room while she was making it. At that time, he was fifteen years old and had just appeared for his tenth-standard Board examinations. He was eagerly awaiting the results which were to be declared in the next month. He had always wanted to be an engineer, like his father. He looked very much like his father too. The same long neck, bushy eyebrows and hollow cheeks. His hair was like Shridhar's but he made no attempt to subdue it. On the contrary, all his efforts seemed to be directed towards making it look untidier. He looked to me very much like a fifteen-year-old boy should. And he had the attitude of a teenager too. He had made a very visible attempt to grow his beard and side-burns. Boys will be boys, teenage boys.

That day, he had a rather grumpy expression on his face. He greeted me but then crossed his arms and sat mute. After a few moments, he started tapping his right foot—which annoyed his grandfather, who gave him a look which made him stop. Some minutes later, he unfolded his hands and started playing the tabla on his knees. Then he ran out of patience and got up and went to the kitchen. Gently touching his mother on the back, he asked her politely if he could help her. He was already taller than her, so she patted him on the shoulder and told him to lay the table and wait. He came back and sat on the sofa again, this time cross-legged. He started rocking back and forth in that position. 'A hungry young man,' I said to myself.

I tried to engage him in conversation to distract him from his hunger. He told me that he had been doing something on the computer. He tried to explain it to me but I felt as though he was speaking in a foreign language.

Rahul's generation is the generation of the computer. He was born in 1989. His father being an engineer and a computer enthusiast himself, a computer entered the household in the late 1990s when they became more common and affordable in India. The children were, of course, forbidden from touching the computer. It was placed in Partha and Anita's bedroom. But Rahul and his sister found ways to sneak in and play on the computer anyway. In a few months, Rahul had become more competent in operating the computer than his father. He even helped his father when the latter had problems with the computer. The fact that he had violated the rules was overlooked. The computer was also moved to Rahul's room. Rahul cannot imagine a life without computers, just like those born ten years after him cannot imagine a life without mobile phones. Little did he know that a time would come when he would not be able to even see a computer for months. But that happened later, much later.

That day, he told me that before his results were out he and his friends would be going for a rafting trip planned by a travel agency. His only regret was that there would be no TV there and he would miss his favourite football club matches. He was a huge fan of Chelsea. Although he liked to play football with his friends, he had a very poor opinion of the Indian football team. He and his friends had never felt like playing football professionally. They preferred to analyze the games and criticize the players for their indiscipline, but couldn't conceive of themselves playing under the guidance of a coach.

Anyway, what is important is that Rahul was a Chelsea fan and, like many other boys of his age and social class, loved Metallica and Hindi movies. He was also a Hindu and, needless to say, knew nothing about Hinduism. But he was a believer. I had asked him once if he believed in God. He had replied, 'Of course, Ajoba, I believe in God, everybody does.' The majority of the people from his social group 'believe' in God and he believes in believing as the majority believes. It is convenient for him to believe in God; it is convenient for all of them. Tomorrow, if being an atheist becomes convenient, Rahul will accept that as well. Such a transition will leave him unperturbed. He doesn't really think about gods or religion. He hardly even remembers their existence, though he swears by them. I call him a Hindu only because he can't be called 'not-Hindu'. He thinks he is a believer. He also believes that 'there are too many fun things to think about in life, so why think about life?'

Rahul did not have to wait too long. All of us went and sat down at the dining table as Anita served us pohe. My favourite breakfast. Shridhar's granddaughter, Janaki, hated pohe, but she had gone out for breakfast with her friends that day so the rest of us could relish the meal without having to look at her annoyed expression. She used to eat pohe in such a way that one felt that she had been asked to eat poison. So her mother avoided serving it as much as possible. How can anyone not like pohe? I still cannot understand it. It's absurd to be born in Maharashtra and not like pohe.

Janaki came home when we had just finished breakfast. She said, 'Hi Ajoba' and smiled. She is fair, tall and the only person in the family to have inherited my friend's eyes and, with them, his myopia. Her eyes were enthusiastic in those days. That particular day, she was surrounded by her family, and her brother was quick to tease her about missing some delightful pohe, for which she rumpled his bushy hair. To her parents' delight, she had not inherited Shridhar's hair. When she was a kid, her mother would plait her long straight hair every day, before she went to school, but the first thing she did when she started to go to college was to cut it short and to get it permed. Till today she still keeps it short, but now she considers it a waste of time to get it permed. At that time, she was just twenty years old, and a student. She is five years older than her brother. Again, unlike her brother, she has chubby cheeks and a stocky neck.

She had completed her BA and wanted to take admission for law at a college in Pune, a task she would accomplish in a few months from that day. Both Shridhar and I had wanted her to be a doctor. I have always believed that she would have become an excellent doctor. She has the correct temperament. When you look at some people you feel calm. At the same time you are aware of the enormous energy they radiate. She is one such person. Thus, both of us never really approved of her reading law. Nevertheless, she had made up her mind to enter that despicable profession, and what gave me more pain was that she was looking forward to it.

From her childhood, I had treated her as my own granddaughter and tried to monopolize her. That is why I believe she invited me to stay with her in Mumbai. And that is why I accepted.

3

MY FRIENDSHIP WITH SHRIDHAR GREW STRONGER AFTER we both got married and had children. Our families used to go together on trips—to Goa, Mahabaleshwar and once, to Rajasthan. My sons and Partha were in the same school. The girls, Sunita and Asha, were in a girls' school. At that time coeducation was not all that common, at least in Pune. When Shridhar's wife passed away, we felt immense grief and my wife especially was very sad. They had developed a very close bond over the years. My sons and Partha are still friends. When they come to Pune they visit him often. They also bring him gifts. They used to bring gifts for Janaki and Rahul too. They used to tell Partha stories about America and how difficult it is for them to look after their children there without any help. They tell him that he is lucky to be living in India—his home country. Then they go back to their sad lives in New Jersey and San Jose to earn more dollars, work in multinational companies and bring more gifts next time from Walmart, Macy's or H&M.

I remember distinctly the births of Partha and his sisters, of Janaki and Rahul, and also their childhoods. After my children went to America, and even more after I retired at the age of sixty-five, my wife and I became frequent visitors at Shridhar's house. As a dentist there was no need for me to retire at sixty-five, but I had wanted to get away from my fixed routine of which I had grown weary. I had earned enough for us in our old age. I had also invested my money and was getting good returns. My children were well settled and we had no need to worry on that account. Thus, after consulting with my wife, I decided to retire to pursue my interest in classical music. To the utter dismay of my children, I began to attend singing classes, a hobby which I continued for a long time. (I call it a hobby as I had never intended to become a professional singer.) I also started attending the music functions which are held regularly in my city.

Thus, our abundant free time allowed my wife and me to become intimately familiar with Shridhar's household. Even before my retirement, we used to visit them regularly and they always invited us to have dinner at their place during Diwali. For Janaki and Rahul, it was as though they had an extra pair of grandparents who would give them gifts and fuss over them.

Childhood is a period in which one learns to trust others instinctively. A few words of comfort, a few gestures and providing a feeling of security are enough to make a child trust you. And that is what made Janaki trust me, a trust that continues till today. I realize that children today are very different from how we were when we were young. And Janaki and Rahul are very different from each other, too. Two incidents from their childhood illustrate that difference.

The first illustrates Janaki's personality. It was also a changing point in my relationship with her. She was a very shy child and hardly spoke in my presence. I had always tried to speak to her, but without much success. I remember I had once said, 'You have such a sweet voice, why don't you talk more? We want to hear you.' To my utter dismay, all I had got as a reply was a nod and smile. She used to consider my wife and me as strangers who came to visit occasionally and would get scared when we tried to fuss over her. That incident changed the way she viewed us and from then she slowly opened up to me, and then to my wife. She stopped being scared of us and started looking forward to our visits. She also started to accompany her grandparents when they came to our house.

She was very young then, in the first or second standard. It was a Saturday and also Shridhar's birthday. I had not retired and thus we went to his house at about eight in the evening, after I'd finished attending to patients. Anita invited us to stay for dinner.

But Janaki was nowhere to be seen. Anita told us that as soon as she had come home at two o'clock that day, she had changed her clothes, eaten her lunch in silence and sat down to do her homework, all without talking. She had not spoken to her mother from the time she came home. Anita had tried to find out what had happened by employing all the means at her disposal, but to no avail. She'd also tried to convince Janaki to go out and play with her friends, but her daughter had insisted that she had to do homework. Janaki's grandmother had cooked her favourite snacks to cheer her up, but she hadn't touched them. Ever since she went into her room to complete her homework, she had come out only once, and that too, to drink milk—something she had always considered equivalent to torture. And, however hard her mother tried to reach out to her, she would not talk. This was very unusual, because usually she would literally spend an hour telling her mother all that had happened in school in detail. Anita would have to force her to start doing her homework. But that day, Janaki studied as long as it was possible for her to study and then she started reading a storybook. All of us were wondering what had gone wrong.

After some time, Anita went to talk to her again. We could hear her speak but we heard no response. In the meantime, Janaki's closest friend, Sandhya, came to meet her, accompanied by her mother. Sandhya was very much like Janaki, shy and calm and a little aloof, but equally energetic. This contrast in characteristics made her personality very interesting. Her thin dark red lips and protruding jaw would have made a person not as shy as her look arrogant. She was slightly plump and a few inches taller than Janaki, with thick, jet black, curly hair, which her mother tied in two plaits. That day, Sandhya, too, seemed to be upset. Her dark eyes had become red from crying and so had her cheeks. She went inside to be with Janaki, while Anita and her mother stayed with us.

Sandhya's mother told us that she had wanted to bring her over earlier, but had been delayed by some visitors to their house. Then she explained what had happened that day in school. Janaki and Sandhya were learning subtraction that day in maths class. The teacher told them that if any number was subtracted from the same number, the remainder would be zero. Janaki had no problem in following this concept. But when the teacher went on to say that zero minus zero is also zero, she was left utterly confused. She found it illogical. She thought that as zero meant 'nothing', any number could not possibly be subtracted from nothing. (She was only in the first or second standard then and was not acquainted with the concept of negative numbers). The idea of subtracting nothing from nothing further confused her, and she requested the teacher to clarify her meaning. Knowing Janaki and how very shy she was, I could imagine that asking a question in front of the whole class must have required a lot of effort on her part and I'm quite sure that she would have been as polite as possible. Unfortunately for Janaki, her question enraged the teacher so much that she threw the duster at her. The very same day, the English teacher had punished Sandhya for a trivial mistake in pronunciation. The girls had just started learning English, but instead of correcting her, the teacher had severely reprimanded Sandhya. The two aggrieved friends had put their heads together and cried.

Sandhya and Janaki spoke to each other in Janaki's room for more than half an hour. Then Sandhya came out of Janaki's bedroom, looking much happier and smiling. The change that the smile brought about on her face was remarkable. A sweet little girl. I have always liked girls more than boys. They seem to be more truthful, more sensitive, and more human.

Sandhya left with her mother and Janaki came out and joined us. She sat next to Anita, who hugged her close. The next day was a Sunday and a holiday from school. Janaki's eyes were still a little red and flashed about the room as we spoke, remnants of her anger. But she soon became herself: calm and shy. We all had dinner, cut a cake and wished Shridhar. After dinner, we sat down again in the living room and I found myself sitting next to Janaki. I patted her head and she looked up at me.

'You are a good girl,' I said. 'And it's not your fault. Don't keep thinking about what you said. And don't think that maybe you shouldn't have asked a question. It's really not your fault.' She smiled. 'Your teacher is…' I shrugged, and then tapped my forehead, shaking my head, and she giggled. I gave her the toffees that I had brought for her. She needed the love and support which her parents and her family gave her. But she also needed an adult to tell her that she was not at fault. And she looked relieved when I did just that, as if a huge burden had been lifted. I think she started trusting me from then. Children are very good judges of character. They understand artificiality instantaneously and are repulsed by it. But if you are truthful, communication with them does not even require words.

Later, I came to know that curiosity is treated as a crime in our school system. Many years after this incident, but while she was still in school, I asked Janaki if the teachers still scolded her.

'No, they don't,' she said with a small smile. 'They can't.'

'Why not,' I asked, and received the answer that I dreaded the most.

'Because we've wised up, all of us,' she answered. 'We don't ask questions any more. We just copy what they tell us and try to understand on our own. For our exams we learn our entire books by heart. What will they punish us for?'

This state of affairs saddens me immensely.

❖

The second incident occurred several years later. Rahul was in the fifth standard at that time and Janaki was in the tenth. They were both in the same school, which had a very good reputation. It was famous for producing toppers in the Board examinations and had a record of hundred per cent passing in the tenth standard. The school building was a fairly conventional modern, tall, structure, but if anybody had told me that it was a factory, or a house for the mentally challenged, that would have sounded quite plausible. The building lacked any sort of character, except that it had an air of being an institution, as opposed to a private residential complex. The only thing that gave it an appearance of being a school was the middle-sized playground in the front. Of course, I had seen the building when it was vacant, when I'd accompanied my younger daughter-in-law for my grandson's admission. The presence of children must have added some life to the building, which the school authorities had, for some peculiar purpose, decided to paint grey.

The building had six floors, with the kindergarten students on the ground floor. There were two staircases, but only one, the side staircase, had windows, which faced the playground. The windows were large and with fixed glazing. From the outside they looked good, but from inside it was not easy to see out. They were set in a niche in the wall, causing a distance of about three to four inches between the stairs and the windows. There were railings just below the niche, so in order to see outside, the older and taller students would lean on the railings. There had been accidents due to this, and the school had strictly prohibited (to Rahul's dismay) all students from making any such attempt.

The school had taken safety precautions. There was an emergency plan in place in case of outbreak of fire or any natural calamity. Emergency drills were conducted annually. The classrooms of the younger children were situated on the lower floors so that they did not have to climb down as much and also to prevent them from being pushed by the elder students if they had to evacuate the school. At both ends of the long passage, there were fire extinguishers. I had been very happy to see all these safety precautions. I shuddered at the memory of my own school. The school building was in a dilapidated condition. In the rainy season it used to leak and we would have to sit in water. Strangely enough I don't remember anyone ever being hurt. We did not feel unsafe either. But that may be because we were not used to safety. So I was very happy when my grandson was admitted there. *Here is a school which cares for its children*, I thought.

My grandson left India soon after. But Janaki and Rahul continued going there. If Janaki had one best friend, Rahul had many friends. He had always been an extroverted and talkative person and made friends very easily and often invited them to his house. My wife and I had often run into them when we visited Shridhar and his wife.

I remember five of them, his closest friends, who formed the core of their group. One of them was a boy called Akshay. He was bespectacled and extremely skinny. There are some children who look naughty and some children who look studious. Akshay belonged to the latter category. He had dark curly hair and large ears which made his face look thinner than it actually was. It looked like an inverted isosceles triangle, the two points at the extremities of his forehead being equidistant from his extremely pointed chin. I had met him often at Shridhar's place and had noticed that he was shy, and because of his chronic bronchitis, seemed frail in comparison to Rahul's sturdy and active frame. In the company of his friends though, and especially of Rahul, he seemed to be very comfortable. He cracked jokes, teased others and allowed himself to be teased. He was less impetuous as compared to Rahul and less hot-headed. He had been Rahul's friend from kindergarten and had, as Rahul himself later admitted, on several occasions restrained Rahul from making mistakes which would certainly not have been forgiven by the school authorities.

For a few months after the incident, Rahul was very disturbed. His behaviour showed such a marked alteration that I asked his mother what had happened. It was from his mother that I learned the facts, which gave me great sorrow. My knowledge was later further supplemented by what Rahul told me himself, once he had returned to being his normal self.

What happened was this. Unlike Rahul, who was very good at sports, Akshay's chronic bronchitis restricted his activities, and he was very good only at his studies. That year, however, he had got bad marks in a series of class tests, a fact which had been troubling him. One day, as schoolchildren often do, Akshay was not paying attention in class. The teacher made him stand and had some very harsh words to say to him. She told him that he was good for nothing, that he was bad at sports and in studies, that he did not have any future and that he was a burden on the school and on his family. She said that the mere fact that he was not paying attention proved his worthlessness and laziness. If he wanted to achieve anything in his life, he had to improve. She said that she wanted to make an example of him and wanted to show the class what would happen to stupid and lazy people like him. Saying this she ordered him to stand for the remaining duration of the period with his hands above his head.

All this happened only because an intelligent boy had got six out of ten in the preceding five class tests. Soon, the fact that the teacher had scolded him spread like wildfire throughout the school to all students and teachers. Every class has an idiot and Akshay was designated as the idiot of the fifth standard. The other teachers started reprimanding him for minor lapses and, even when he had not done anything wrong at all, began making snide remarks about him in passing. Naturally, other students started making fun of him too. Throughout all this, Rahul stood up for Akshay and offered him support, even at the cost of losing some of his other friends.

One day, the class-teacher gave Akshay a note for his parents which said that he had not been studying properly and it was high time for his parents to discipline him. Akshay did not give the note to his parents. The next day, when the teacher questioned him, he told her that he had lost the note. The teacher reprimanded him for his carelessness and gave him another note, warning him that if he lost it this time, she would call up his parents and that the school principal herself would punish him.

Akshay sat with Rahul during the lunch break that day but he didn't speak at all. Rahul tried to cheer him up, unsuccessfully. Just five minutes before the end of the break, Akshay got up and hugged Rahul, thanking him and apologizing for being a lousy friend. Ignoring Rahul's protests, he left him, saying he needed to go to the toilet before the next class.

Rahul didn't realize anything was wrong, until Akshay didn't turn up even after the bell for the next class had rung. Then, he got worried. The same teacher who had first scolded Akshay was scheduled to deliver the lecture and Rahul was scared that if Akshay turned up late he would be severely punished.

Akshay had actually not gone to the toilet at all. He had gone to the sixth floor, which housed only the botany and chemistry labs, and so was usually deserted during the break. Though there were fire extinguishers on every floor, those on the fifth and sixth floors were empty. This was common knowledge amongst the students, as they had been empty for years. Akshay was able to easily lift the fire extinguisher from its place, and put it into the window niche. He must have stepped on the staircase railing to heave himself into the window niche, alongside the extinguisher. Using it to break the window, he jumped from the sixth floor. He committed suicide.

Rahul was devastated by the death of his dearest friend. He hit back in the only way he knew, throwing ink and chalk at the teachers and putting glue on their seats so that their saris would get stuck and tear. He started bunking lectures and disrupting any class he attended by talking loudly and squirting water from his bottle on the other students and their books. This time, there was no Akshay to control his behaviour and calm him down. He was suspended from school for two weeks with a warning that if these antics continued, he would be rusticated.

A student taking his own life scared all the parents. They blamed the school for not taking proper care, for not providing proper supervision. The Pune City edition of the regional newspaper carried the news of Akshay's suicide on the front page and severely criticized the principal for not looking after the safety of the students. The school administration issued a written apology to the parents, promising to ensure that the requisite measures were taken. The extinguishers on the top two floors were replaced and the windows were fitted with iron grilles so that no one would be able to jump through them. Students were thereafter prohibited from standing anywhere near the staircases or going on the roof. The same newspaper carried a list of these measures, and the parents felt reassured that their children were safe. Nobody cared to try and understand what drove that particular young boy to commit suicide.

When I first heard of Akshay's death, I, too, was shocked. The life of an innocent boy had been lost, because of a system which gives importance only to marks. A system so competitive that it destroys all human relations. This system cannot be called a school. It can only be called a factory, meant to produce engineers and doctors, for it considers all other professions unimportant. But this factory system continues because parents support it. They don't want their children to be scientists or thinkers or writers or artists or painters. They all just want their children to stand first in class. For Akshay's death I blame his parents equally. If he had been in a position to show that note at home he would not have died.

In the last two decades, suicides amongst students have risen alarmingly. At first, I used to blame the system totally, but then I sat back and analyzed the situation. When we were young, we also suffered under the same system. Our teachers used language which was much more abusive, and almost always accompanied their scolding with severe physical punishments. Our parents didn't coddle us much either. They used to occasionally receive reports about our performance from our teachers and if we dared to contradict these reports, we would be at the receiving end of another sound thrashing, this time at the hands of our fathers.

When I compare my childhood to Rahul's or Akshay's or Janaki's, these children seem to have it much better. They certainly receive far more material comforts than we ever did. I started wondering, has the middle and upper-middle class made its children too soft? Are they so accustomed to justice that they cannot tolerate injustice? While trying to give their children better lives than they themselves had, have middle-class parents made their children so ignorant of the outside world that they misjudge the severity of their own problems and over-react? And have I, as a person belonging to the middle class, and as a parent, thus done a great disservice to my children?

In our country, some children are forced to fight diseases that are mere names to our children. These children fight when they are just moments away from death. They lie in their beds, in government hospitals which have neither enough staff nor enough medicines, and fight till their last breath. And they die. Children who do not come from poor families, but from middle-class ones like Akshay's, have begun to die too, albeit from a different cause. Is that due to the failure of their parents to expose them to life outside the comforts of their house? The world we inherited was no better than the world they have inherited, I reflected, but we were more aware of the outside world. We were less protected.

But then I remember that I have forgotten one variable. That is this system, at school and at home, which tells small children that their life has value only if they come first. Even doing well is not good enough; only coming first is acceptable. It expects them to be machines, with no individual talents, aptitudes or interests. It forces them to run, harder and harder, perform better than their capacity. And it creates machines best trained to make maximum money after leaving school. Machines that are unconcerned about anything other than money.

And those who don't do well? Well, they don't deserve to survive then. Isn't this school system a reflection of our wider social system?

After his suspension, Rahul's parents took him to a counsellor but he refused to speak to her. It was Janaki who spent as much time as possible with Rahul during his suspension and finally managed to communicate with him. He refused to speak to anyone in the beginning, but Janaki persisted. She was also affected by Akshay's death and shared his grief. She did not tell him to calm down or to forget and move on, but encouraged him to talk and tell her how he felt. When he finally did, she understood and supported his anger. She even defended him when his parents tried to tell him that creating disturbances in class was wrong. Janaki provided a space where he could vent his anger without fear of reproach. Slowly, his pain and anger became more manageable, and Janaki encouraged him to return to the counsellor.

When Rahul went back to school, he did not disrupt the classes or attack the teachers, but he remained aloof and withdrawn. He did not talk with his other friends and ate his meals alone. His bubbly and outgoing personality became withdrawn. Time heals all wounds, they say. And it's true that after intensely talking to his sister, and many therapy sessions, Rahul eventually became his talkative and friendly self again, making many new friends. However, he has continued to harbour a very deep dislike for the system which, he believes, murdered his friend.

Janaki's and Rahul's responses to what they perceived as injustice were radically different. While Janaki withdrew within herself, Rahul retaliated and stood up against it. Of course, Rahul's close friend had died and that must have had a much greater impact on him. But their whole approach was different. While Janaki did not think of retaliating and suffered in silence, Rahul wanted to teach a lesson to those who had hurt his friend. He resisted, but his resistance lacked any direction or planning. It was completely based on emotions, a passionate response in the heat of the moment. When he came to terms with Akshay's death, his resistance ended. This was because it was a blindly emotional response, not based on any intellectual analysis of what went wrong. He blamed the system for his friend's death but did not analyze it. If his friend had not died but had continued to suffer in silence, he would not even have questioned why the teachers picked out a scapegoat to attack. Janaki, on the other hand, understood the system much better. By no longer asking questions in class, she understood that she could protect herself. It is not always possible for a child to stand up to adults, but she did not do so even when she could have, in small ways. She proved herself to be far too malleable.

4

As Janaki grew older, she slowly started to open up. I found myself wanting to spend time with her. I loved listening to her sweet voice; we used to just sit and I would listen to her talk, about anything and everything. We used to talk about her school, about her friends—especially about Sandhya—about butterflies and her favourite subjects, about Faster Fene the boy detective and Sherlock Holmes, about her favourite cricketers and movie actors.

One Sunday, my wife and I were invited to Shridhar's house for dinner. Janaki must have been in the third standard then and was about eight years old. As we were leaving our house, the neighbours spotted us and came out. We had known them ever since we had moved into the building, more than fifteen years earlier. They invited us in for a cup of tea, as their son was getting married the next month. Although we were getting late, we accepted on the condition that we would not stay for long. But by the time we left their house with the invitation card in our hands, we were already an hour late. When we finally reached, Anita opened the door and let us in.

'Doctor, where were you? I was starting to get worried,' said Shridhar, getting up from his armchair.

I told him the reason for the delay as we settled down, and accepted a glass of water from Anita. I took a sip and then, noticing that Janaki was not around, asked where she was.

'She says she doesn't want to talk to you,' replied Shridhar with a smile.

'Why? What happened?' I exclaimed, rather surprised.

'She has been waiting for you for a long time,' explained Shridhar's wife. 'She wanted to show you a new dance step that she learnt in class today. She waited and waited for you. We even called your house, but no one picked up. So she was very disappointed, and now she is sitting in her room and she doesn't want to talk to anyone. She is not even allowing anyone to come inside the room, except Rahul.'

'I had no idea,' I said truthfully. 'If we had known this, we would have come immediately. We just couldn't avoid talking with our neighbours.'

But then I felt a pang of guilt as I remembered that the last time I had met Janaki, she had told me that she had joined Bharatnatyam classes. It had taken a lot of persuasion before she had promised to show me what she had learnt the next time I met her. I had forgotten this conversation, but she must have remembered it, for she had waited for me, to show me her dance steps.

'Can I please meet her?' I said.

'Sure,' replied Anita. 'But she is very angry, and she is a very stubborn girl. I don't know if she will talk. Please try to convince her.'

'Well, let's see,' I replied. 'The fault is mine.' And we followed her into Janaki's room.

Janaki was sitting on her bed and Rahul was next to her. He must have been about four years old at that time. They were playing with a puzzle. When we entered, Rahul smiled and came running to hug us. I picked him up and sat on the bed next to Janaki. She would not look at me and refused to answer to her name. I handed Rahul to his mother and she took him outside.

'Janaki, we are so sorry. We are really really sorry,' I said

My wife came and sat on the other side of Janaki and said, 'We didn't think you'd be waiting for us, dear. If we had known, we would never have made you wait.'

But Janaki still refused to look at us. I gestured to my wife, indicating that I wanted to talk to Janaki alone, and she quietly patted Janaki's hand and left. I placed my hand under Janaki's chin and gently turned her head up. Her eyes were red.

'I am really so sorry. I convinced you to show me the dance steps you had learnt and then I came late and made you wait. Come on, please forgive me. At least give me a smile. At least look at me,' I said, patting her shoulder.

She glanced up at me, but briefly and with anger.

'Will you show me your dance now?' I asked

'Never.' She shook her head without looking at me.

'Okay. If you show me your dance, I promise I'll also dance for you and you can laugh at me as much as you want,' I continued.

She gave a small smile. I placed my hand on her back and waited. After a moment, she looked up at me, properly. 'I was waiting for you. I waited for you for so long,' she said stormily, her eyes filling with tears of anger. 'I practised because I wanted to show you the steps. And you didn't come. I wanted to show you my dance.'

'Well, you can show me now,' I said.

'Never.' She took off her glasses and dried her eyes.

I tried to hug her. She pushed me away at first, saying,

'I hate you, I hate you.' But as she started crying, she buried her face between my neck and shoulders and allowed me to hug her, while at the same time pounding my chest with her little fists.

That day, I realized how much she cared about me. And, seeing how much pain I felt as she cried, I also realized how much I cared for her. Ever since, I have tried to minimize her pain, however I could. But then there came a time when I could only stand by helplessly.

After she calmed down, she did dance for me, but refused to come outside and dance in front of everyone. I also kept my promise and danced in front of her, as she laughed at me. When we rejoined the rest of the party in the living room she was in a much better mood and the dinner passed off rather happily.

Another night about two years later. It was August 1995, and about a week after Janaki's tenth birthday. We had invited Shridhar and his wife to our house for dinner, and Janaki was supposed to accompany them. But when they came Janaki was not there. Bored of being cooped up in the house due to the rains, Janaki had gone with Sandhya to the playground directly opposite their building. When her grandparents came to pick her up, she was covered in mud and rainwater, but bright-eyed and excited. They told her to go home and wash up, and it was decided that she would accompany her parents to their friends' house, later in the evening. I was a bit disappointed not to see her, but it was also satisfying to talk to my old friend and his wife without any children around.

Just as we were about move to the dining room for dinner, the phone rang. It was Anita, wanting to speak to Shridhar's wife. We all lingered in the living room and couldn't help overhearing her side of the conversation. Anita explained something, and she responded, 'Oh. But she is not with us...'

She was beginning to look a little perturbed as Anita spoke, but she responded, 'Yes, but since she was so dirty, we dropped her off at the bottom of the stairs... We told her to go with you instead; we were getting late and...'

'But we thought you were still at home... The car was there, so...'

By now, she was quite worried. 'No, no, she is not here! We thought she is with you...'

'Okay, we are also coming,' she said and put down the phone abruptly.

Answering our questioning looks she said, 'Janaki is not with them.'

Shridhar and she again began explaining that they had dropped Janaki at their home and had seen her parents' car parked in its usual spot.

'We'll discuss that later. First, let's find her,' I interjected. 'If she is not at home, she must have gone back to the playground after you left. Let's go and bring her home.'

We all left hurriedly for their house in my car. As we parked, we met Anita and Partha, returning from their friend's house. The same kind of dialogue ensued again, with both parents and grandparents explaining why they'd thought Janaki had been with the others.

'What if she had a seizure?' Anita interupted, her face betraying her terror.

On hearing this, I froze. I had almost forgotten that Janaki suffered from benign epilepsy, a mild form in which epileptic seizures can be averted by taking medication. However, the medicines have to be taken regularly for a fixed period of time and during this period, the seizures can recur. Janaki had not yet completed the three-year-long medication period and so the recurrence of the seizures was a very real possibility.

Trying to regain control of my emotions, I said. 'She will be fine. She hasn't had any seizures for the last two years. We shouldn't waste any more time. Let's go and check the playground first. She might have gone back there.'

Rahul, who had by this time realized that his sister was missing and the matter was serious, started crying. His grandmother waited with him in the car as we searched for Janaki at the playground. There were puddles everywhere and the ground had become slippery. It was fully dark by now, and we could not see properly despite the overhead lights at the four corners of the playground.

We saw a couple of young boys sitting in one corner. They were looking at something on the ground and talking rather animatedly and laughing. Their clothes were torn and they were covered with mud. As they saw us approaching, they stood up and one of them put something in his pocket. As we got closer to them, they exchanged glances and then suddenly they fled. Partha ran after them, but they were too quick for him. Their running away distressed us even more, and Anita started crying.

'She'll be all right. We'll find her,' I said, trying to sound confident. No one replied.

When we had finished searching the playground twice, we decided that there was no point in spending more time there.

'Let's call the hospital,' Anita said.

'There's no point in calling them up. We have to find her first,' Partha replied.

'Then let's at least call the police,' she pleaded.

'Check the entire area first,' I advised them. 'Then if she is not there, we'll go to the police.'

We continued searching up and down the lanes near Shridhar's house, but with no result. It was almost ten thirty by that time and I could feel the tension rise. Even if she had not had a seizure, I still did not want to think of the things that could happen to a ten-year-old girl alone on the streets so late.

The watchman of Shridhar's apartment woke up because of our calls and came out to ask us what had happened. He said he hadn't seen Janaki at all that evening and returned to his post. But I could see that Anita did not trust him because he was a Bihari migrant.

'Maybe we should check with Sandhya's parents,' suggested my wife. 'Could Janaki have gone to their house?'

As we headed to Sandhya's, I could feel the heaviness growing in my heart. On the steps of the house, suddenly Anita froze in her tracks. 'Rahul! Where is Rahul,' she exclaimed, looking if possible more frightened.

'He is with his Aaji... remember?' Partha replied. 'They

are sitting in the car. I'll go and drop them home. You speak to Sandhya's parents; I'll be back in a minute.' Saying this, Partha raced downstairs.

Sandhya's mother told us that she hadn't seen Janaki that day, but thought that her daughter might have some idea about what Janaki had been planning to do. She went to wake her up and we waited outside. Suddenly, we heard footsteps hurrying up the stairs, and Shridhar's wife appeared, panting out that they had found Janaki, and she was safely at their house! The relief was indescribable, but we all had so many questions about what she had been doing. I suggested that Anita and my wife should go back to meet Janaki, while I told Sandhya's mother that she had been found.

After informing Sandhya's mother and a sleepy and confused Sandhya that Janaki had been found, I went to Shridhar's house. Janaki was sitting in her bedroom with her parents and she was unhurt. No seizures. Her grandmother had found Janaki sleeping on the sofa when she entered the house. Partha had woken her up and she had become very agitated, and had started crying on seeing them. They still didn't have any idea what she had been doing, or how she had got into the locked house after everyone had left.

We eventually pieced the story together. Janaki had indeed been left at the entrance to the house by her grandparents while her parents were still at home. But she had been scared that they would scold her for getting so dirty and so she had entered the house quietly from the balcony attached to her room. When her mother had locked up the house before leaving, Janaki had been in the bathroom, silently cleaning up. By the time she came out, she had found the house deserted. The front door was locked from the outside and all the balcony doors had been locked from the inside. She did not have the strength to open their wooden doors, because they had swelled with the rains and were too firmly jammed in the frames for her to move them. She had tried to shout out of the window, but nobody had heard her. She had thought about calling my house, but she did not know the phone number. At that time there were no mobiles, so there was no way for her to reach her parents. She had waited for a long time for someone to come home, getting very hungry and scared, but in the end she had fallen asleep on the couch in the living room.

Janaki's parents were sitting with her, inside her room. When Partha came out to gulp down a glass of water, he placed his hands on the table, bent his head down and gave a sigh. I could see the lingering tension in his body, overlaid by relief at finding Janaki safe. Then he went back into the room. I could hear Anita singing in a soothing, soft voice. When she stopped, Janaki said something to her and she started singing another song. At the end, Partha also joined in. Afterwards, he said something to Janaki and I could hear her quiet voice replying. Then Anita came out and told me that Janaki wanted to talk to me. It was almost midnight, so I was surprised, but very happy that she had thought of me.

When I went inside, I realized that the bedroom must have been witness to a mini-tantrum. Two pillows were lying on the floor at opposite ends of the room and a chair was lying on its back. Her school bag had been flung into a corner where it lay, all her books spilling out of it and her toys seemed to have been most unceremoniously thrown around the room. Janaki was lying on her bed, with her head in her mother's lap. She was not asleep, but not entirely awake either. I could see the sleep in her eyes. I patted her head and she smiled. She opened her eyes and said, 'Ajoba'. Then she took both my hands in hers and fell asleep. I sat there, looking at her, hoping that she would never have to face any difficulty or pain in life. I kissed her on the forehead. I removed her glasses and kept them on the side table and tucked her in her blanket.

This incident shook every one up, especially Janaki's parents. After she had gone to sleep, all of us sat down in the living room and tried to relax—except Anita, who kept going back into the children's room to check on her. Shridhar was clearly relieved, but though he sat back in his chair with his eyes closed, the hours of strain showed on his face.

For me, finding her safe and sound did not lead to a release from fear. In fact, I felt a new kind of fear, for the first time. When I was in college I used to walk through all kinds of roads at night without being scared. And what could have really happened to me? Even later in life, I had never felt this sort of dread. I don't have a daughter. For the first time I was scared of the road at night.

After a few days, everyone forgot about that night. But we were all going to be forced to remember it years later, and in much more dire circumstances.

5

THE SATURDAY AFTER JANAKI'S EIGHTEENTH BIRTHDAY, we had gone to Shridhar's house for dinner. In the morning, both of us had congratulated Janaki on becoming an adult over the phone. When we reached their house, her mother told us that she had celebrated her birthday with her college friends that year, and was out relishing a meal of pani puri and bhel with Sandhya. When Shridhar and I were young, pani puri was not as popular in Pune. Misal was and still is the favourite snack of all Punekars. But sometimes, when we were not all that hungry, we used to eat bhel. Our school was situated in the inner part of the old city and every Saturday was a half day. Whenever we could get our hands on some money, we used walk to a small hill called Parvati to eat bhel. We would share one plate and our stomachs would be full. But by the time we walked, or rather ran, the two kilometres back to our homes, we used to be hungry again.

We were finishing dinner when Janaki returned. 'Sandhya just gave me this jacket,' she said, answering her mother's questioning look at her brand-new pink jacket. 'Isn't it gorgeous?' she added happily.

When we gave her our present, she was delighted. We had deliberated for some time about what we should buy her. In the end, we decided we should present her with a gift coupon from Crosswords bookstore. She loved reading. I found her very peculiar in that sense. When she was happy, she read. When she was sad, she read. When she was tense, she preferred to read. And when she was bored, she read! To each her own…

She was, as expected, childishly giddy at becoming an adult. She started teasing Rahul, who had turned thirteen that year, reminding him at every possible opportunity that he was still 'legally' a child. This fact seemed to hurt him and Janaki added fuel to the fire. Every person who has an elder sibling has suffered this agony. I have, too. However old you get, they are still older than you. If you become an adolescent, they are one step ahead of you, they are adults. If you want to rejoice that you are about to complete college, they remind you that they already have jobs. But sometimes this race between siblings gets evened out in old age, when they start getting grey hair before you!

Rahul was facing a similar situation. He had just become a teenager, only a month earlier and his elder sister, or Tai as he called her, was not allowing him to cherish that fact, since she had become an adult. She told him that now she had the right to vote, to enter into contracts (a sign of her inclination towards the legal profession which I should have noticed) and to marry. That last was not a good example, as it gave Rahul ammunition to tease her back. 'Yes,' he chuckled, 'now we have to find a groom for you immediately.'

'I am not going to get married, ever,' said Janaki, waving her hands to underline her point.

'You can't say that anymore,' said Rahul with a smirk. 'In a few days, when you come from college, you'll find that a guy and his family have come to see you and fix a match. And then, in a few months you'll be "legally" married,' he added gleefully.

'Never, never, never,' Janaki shouted at him. 'Shut up or you'll get a beating,' she added rolling back her sleeve and making an intimidating fist.

'Okay, okay, I'll shut up. Don't get angry,' he said patronisingly. But obviously he was not going to let it go.

After a short pause he added, soberly and without making eye contact with Janaki, 'My shutting up is not going to change anything, you know.'

She gave him an annoyed look which he ignored as he turned to me, saying cheerfully, 'Can you imagine, Ajoba, what a catastrophe the ceremony of presenting her for marriage will be? After all, Tai does not like to eat pohe and cannot make it.'

I couldn't help smiling, for pohe is, indeed, the snack usually offered for such functions and I remembered her annoyed expressions every time she realized that she had to eat it.

'Well, you don't need to worry about any catastrophe,' she responded thoughtfully. 'You're a child. Children should not have to bear the burdens of the family.'

Rahul steered the conversation again towards the topic of her marriage and their banter continued. Every person who has a sibling or even cousins with whom they have grown up is accustomed to playing this game, part banter, part true needling. It is our first test at patience and perseverance and it can go on and on for hours or even days. Anita, of course, was long familiar with it and considered it best to stop them then and there. She told both of them to abstain from teasing each other, saying to Rahul, 'Being an adult is really not that great. And, anyway, you only have five years left.'

From the expression on his face, it was obvious that 'only' was not the word that Rahul associated with five years. But he did drop the topic.

Then Anita said to Janaki, 'And you don't need to worry about getting married so soon. You are just eighteen. There is still time for you to get married. We will see when the time is right. You'll also want to get married by then, and...'

'No, I won't,' Janaki interrupted.

'We'll see when we get there, okay?' her mother said smilingly and the conversation stopped there. But Janaki did not seem satisfied.

Some time had passed since we had finished dinner. It had begun to rain outside. When Janaki offered to make coffee, everyone liked the idea better than Shridhar's offer of tea just a few minutes before. Anita offered to make the coffee instead, as it was still so close to Janaki's birthday, but instead of thanking her mother, Janaki snapped at her, insisting that she alone would make the coffee. After a few minutes, we heard the crash of utensils falling, followed by a hasty 'I'm fine, no need to come in here' from Janaki. Anita had already got up, though she looked more resigned than alarmed, but I signalled to her that I'd go and check if everything was indeed all right.

In the kitchen, Janaki was picking up the utensils from the floor and muttering to herself. When she saw me, she gave a brief smile and continued putting the utensils back into the cupboard.

'And this is how the utensils should be stacked!' she said,

slamming the door shut. Seeing my puzzled expression, she explained, 'Our cook stacks all the utensils on each other in such a way that it is almost impossible to open the door without them all falling out. My mother has told her so many times not to arrange the utensils this way, but it's no use.'

Well, that explains Anita's expression when she heard the noise, I thought. But looking at Janaki's thunderous face, I wondered if the cook's carelessness was the sole reason for the falling of the utensils, for she seemed to have carried her foul mood into the kitchen. She had filled a pot with water, which she slammed onto the gas stove with such force that some of the water splashed out. She added a little more to it with a cup, and then tried to ignite the gas in such a hurry that it did not catch. I took the lighter from her hand and turned off the gas. After waiting for a few moments for the gas fumes to clear, I lit the burner.

She sniffed and then, without looking at me, said, 'Thank you.'

'Are you all right?' I asked.

'Yes,' she snapped.

It was the first time that she was cooking anything for us and I thought perhaps that she had become nervous because I had come into the kitchen. I thought it was best to start a conversation on some different topic so that she could relax.

'Your cousin Siddhartha is getting married next month, isn't he?' I asked. I knew him because he was a patient of mine and a rather regular one, visiting me every time he came home to Pune from his IT job in the south. His teeth are among the worst I have seen in my career.

'Yeah,' she answered, still not looking at me. After a short pause, she added, 'I'm going to wear a sari.' There was a hint of pride in her voice. She told me that she had worn a sari only once before and that she was looking forward to this occasion. Youngsters today have to look for occasions for wearing saris, while in our youth women hardly had any other choice. I remembered how uncomfortable my mother had looked when she had first worn a salwar-kameez.

'How times have changed,' I said regretfully. She hadn't met my eyes yet, but had seemed a little more relaxed while talking about dressing up for the wedding. Now, she seemed annoyed again. I myself have adopted completely Western attire and have never worn anything other than shirts and pants, so who was I to say anything to her? Maybe it was better to keep talking about the wedding. 'I have been invited too,' I informed her.

'I know, Aba told me,' she replied.

The atmosphere had become very uncomfortable and our verbal exchanges seemed unnatural, if not outright ridiculous. She had never been so withdrawn around me since I first saw her come out of her shell when she was in first standard. After a few moments of silence between us, as though feeling a need to keep me entertained, she continued the same topic.

'He has a very good job in Bangalore. He's thirty-five years old, but he wasn't ready to get married till now. He had too much work and hardly any time to spare. But now he has more time. His parents were getting worried. She also works in the same sector, same company. Now they are relieved,' she said, with no interest in her voice, still refusing to make eye contact with me.

'Yes, I can imagine how worried his parents must have been,' I said just to keep the conversation flowing, and at the same time remembering the marriages of my own two sons. 'But nowadays it is bound to happen,' I added. 'There is nothing wrong in having a good career. And today, education goes on for a long time. By the time you are settled and you start earning properly, you're thirty. He is an intelligent chap. He is getting married before it is too late.'

'Yes, that's true. There is some age difference between them. She is twenty-nine and he is thirty-five,' she said, finally looking at me. She shrugged and said, 'but that's okay.'

'Yes, they will manage,' I said, but I was perturbed by the news. I couldn't contain myself, so I added: 'Twenty-nine is a bit too old though. Girls don't usually remain unmarried for so long.' She didn't respond.

'Everything is changing,' I added after a while with a sigh. 'We are becoming unnecessarily individualistic. No one cares about children or family anymore. Parents are too busy with their own careers.'

'I thought you said that there is nothing wrong in giving importance to "career",' she said, looking at me sternly.

'Yes, that's true,' I said, hesitantly. 'But …'

'But it doesn't apply to women, does it?' she asked with a weary smile.

'That's not true,' I said, rather offended at such an accusation. 'Both my daughters-in-law work …'

'And they stopped working when they had children,' she said in a constricted voice. 'Now the children are grown up, so they work part-time. You call yourself progressive because you "allow" your daughters to have jobs. But you don't want them to have careers, do you? You want us to be just mothers, my mother wants me to be just a mother…'

'And is there anything wrong with being a mother?' I asked politely after a few moments. 'Why are you so against it?'

'Because I hate children. I hate them, okay? Children are the basis of our bloody patriarchal system. I was not born to be only a mother. Am I not a person? Don't I have an identity? I want grow, to develop to the best of my capacity. I want to understand the world that we live in. And I want to understand who I am. You're suffocating me. You're trying to kill me. And I won't let you do that.'

There was a stunned silence for a moment. I did not know what to say. She stood with her arms crossed defensively across her chest, breathing quickly. When she resumed speaking, her voice sounded harsh. 'Love for children is compulsory for women, and voluntary for men. You men don't have emotions. And that helps, doesn't it? Emotions just make you weak.'

'And is being strong all that matters?' I argued. 'Your concept of strength is flawed if it means that you have to stop feeling, have to stop being human. Is that why you are opposed to marriage?' There was an uncomfortable pause.

I sighed. 'I may have applied double standards to men and women, Janaki, but that's not because I want to exploit anyone. You may call me prejudiced—and you may be right to some extent. But please consider what I am going to say. I want you to know that as long as I live, I will always respect and support your choice. But give yourself the right to change if you feel like it. Don't take decisions on the basis of your conception of strength. Don't plan for your entire life.'

'Thanks, Ajoba,' she said in a composed voice. She turned off the stove, poured the coffee into mugs and left, saying, 'I'll take this out for everyone.'

I stayed inside, perturbed, and thinking about what she had said. Have I been a good husband to my wife who is sitting outside? Have I ever asked my wife what she wanted to do with her life? I had always assumed that looking after the family was what she wanted. I don't even know what marriage had stopped her from doing. But then, why didn't she resent me? Maybe even she did not believe that she had a choice, that she could have had a life outside the house. Or maybe she had reconciled herself to her fate to reduce the pain of her dreams being shattered. Did I really know anything about my life partner? A person who knew me in every particular, who knew my every wish and desire, every habit and character?

And what about being a father? Had I been a bad father too? Not true, I reminded myself. I spent more time with them than many other fathers do.

But I was also worried about Janaki and how she had behaved. Her sudden outburst just now—it was very uncharacteristic. She was usually always the same calm, shy, composed girl. Not one to slam doors, but one who would distribute each cup of coffee with a small smile. It disturbed me to think that she could have so much anger hidden under her smile. But maybe it was just a spurt of ill-temper, not something deep.

I heard Rahul say something outside, but Janaki did not reply. She came back into the kitchen and slammed down the tray. In her eyes, I saw fury. 'What happened?' I asked.

'Nothing,' she replied. Then, after a pause, 'Rahul was saying that if I take so much time to make coffee, any family which comes to see me for marriage will fall asleep by the time I deliver it to them.'

By then, Rahul had entered the kitchen as well. He had realized that he had upset her and was looking remorseful and concerned. Janaki's back was turned towards him as she wiped up the water around the stove. He looked at me and I nodded to indicate that he should speak to her. 'Sorry, Tai,' he said in a low voice, touching her back. When she did not respond, he continued, 'I didn't want to upset you. I thought it was just a game, the same banter as earlier. I didn't mean any of what I said.'

'It's okay,' she said sniffling. He looked at her in alarm and she responded to his expression with a rather teary-eyed smile, saying, 'Kids make such errors in judgement. You are only a teenager after all.'

They both started laughing, and the next instant they were mock-boxing and throwing water on each other. As I shepherded them out of the kitchen, I could not help smiling.

6

DIWALI IS MY FAVOURITE FESTIVAL. WHEN WE WERE YOUNG, Shridhar and I used to celebrate it together. As time passed, we started celebrating it with our families. But we used to always visit each other during Diwali.

Then things changed. My sons grew up and immigrated to America. They still call me on Diwali though, and they celebrate it themselves as much as possible. After that, Partha's sisters got married and left for their own homes. Partha got married and Janaki and Rahul were born. My wife died and so did Shridhar's. Partha and Anita had their own friends and relatives.

I was invited to Shridhar's house for lunch and dinner more than once during the Diwali of 2006, but I thought it better not to go as my presence may have discomfited their friends and relatives, especially those from Anita's side. Thus, when the doorbell rang on the last evening of Diwali, and I saw it was Shridhar, I was overwhelmed and delighted. I was even more surprised that Janaki was with him.

Shridhar told me that he had wanted to meet me. He had been sure that I would be home, because I myself had told him a few days earlier that I did not want to go visiting any more of my relatives, to rest my ageing bones—and also my ageing stomach, which needed to be protected from an overdose of the delicious and irresistible delicacies that Diwali brings. He told me that Partha and Anita had gone to visit her sister who lived in the old city and that Rahul was at home, studying. He was in the twelfth standard then, and wanted to become an engineer, so he was having to study really hard to get admission in a good college.

I had learnt from Rahul himself some time before that there were a ludicrous number of examinations to give. First came Maharashtra's twelfth standard Board examinations. 'But those are not that important,' Rahul had said. The important exams, on the basis of which admission was given, were the CET, the MH-CET and the IIT entrance exams. Of these, the last were probably the most important, as they determined admission for some of the most prestigious engineering institutions in the country. To prepare for this barrage of examinations, Rahul was attending four different tuition classes. The tuition centres were, of course, shut for the five days of Diwali, but the teachers had given such preposterous quantities of homework that Rahul did not even have time to devour the delicacies prepared by his mother and Janaki. This year, Janaki had insisted that her mother teach her how to make them, a request which was immediately and very happily fulfilled.

Thus, Rahul was still finishing his homework. Janaki, on the other hand, was free. As Shridhar reported to me rather sorrowfully, she was enjoying her studies. She was in the second year of law and, although she was doing an internship at a law firm, she had holidays for Diwali. Her college wouldn't open for another two weeks.

'Why didn't Janaki go to her aunt's place with her parents?' I asked Shridhar after he had settled down in his favourite chair in my house.

'Don't know,' said Shridhar shrugging. 'Where is she anyway,' he added, craning his neck to look for her.

'I saw her go to the balcony, I think,' I replied. When Janaki was young, she used to often accompany Shridhar and his wife to my house. The first time she came, she wandered about the house. On her second visit, she discovered the balcony at the other end of the house. Ever since, whenever she would come, she would sit there, for some time at least.

'She was going to visit Madhuri,' said Shridhar, interrupting my train of thought and bringing me back to the present. 'But then she decided that she didn't want to go there. She said she would come with me. Her mother got very angry, but she just wouldn't listen. I have no idea what happened. She was fine earlier, in the morning, but later seemed upset about something. Must have fought with Rahul. They are always fighting. This is an important year for Rahul. Can't she just leave him alone? But no, she is always fighting with him. This has all started since she joined that law college…

'I just stay away from it all. I am too old now. I didn't ask her why she changed her mind; I just brought her along. I knew you'd be pleased to have her.'

'Yes. It's been years since she last came, hasn't it?' I said fondly.

'Yes, but she hasn't changed,' he smiled. 'She's still fond of your balcony.'

That day was Janaki's first visit to my house since my wife had died, almost two years ago. Usually when children grow up, it is the parents and grandparents who feel the loss of their company most severely. With Janaki, I felt it too. I didn't live with her, but I enjoyed having conversations with her whenever I visited Shridhar. As she started spending less time at home, my opportunities to talk with her were naturally curtailed. But she had to grow up. And I knew that she remembered and trusted me in the same way she had when she was in school. The only change was that the ambit of her experiences and relationships had increased.

Shridhar and I kept talking for some time, as old friends do. I told him how my youngest grandson had sent me a photo of himself wearing a kurta for Diwali. He swore that he would follow my example the next year and not visit his family during the festivities. 'I get tired,' he said with a sigh. 'My bones have become old now,' he added, patting his biceps. After some time though, Shridhar wanted to watch his favourite TV serial. I only watch the news, but I knew that Shridhar was very particular about his serial, so I turned on the TV and handed him the remote. He smiled like a toddler presented with his favourite toy. Soon, he was engrossed and, sensing that he would not miss my presence, I got up and went to the balcony.

Janaki was standing there, looking at the lane below. My apartment is on the fourth floor, away from the main road and the noise. The sun was about to set and it was beginning to get dark. I stood looking at her for a moment. She was staring down, apparently deep in thought. The wind was blowing softly, playing with her short hair which just grazed her shoulders. She was wearing her favourite pink jacket, Sandhya's gift on her eighteenth birthday. I remembered how she used to stand in the balcony when she was younger, clinging to the railing because she was afraid of heights, but at the same time insisting that she wanted to see what was happening below. I used to give her a toffee every time for being a brave girl. My wife used to buy different coloured fruit toffees and we always had a batch at home. But that day I had none, and I couldn't help regretting it. 'If only I had known,' I said to myself. 'But she is too old to eat toffees now, anyway.' Still, old habits die hard.

That year, Diwali had come in late October, so there was a slight chill in the air. Suddenly she shivered and rubbed her palms and then placed them on her cheeks. Realizing I was there, she turned and said, 'Hi, Ajoba,' with a smile.

'Hi,' I replied, 'Our tradition is going to be broken, Janaki.'

She raised her eyebrows.

'That of standing in the balcony and sucking toffees,' I explained.

'No worries, Ajoba,' she said, taking two toffees from her jacket pocket. She handed me one.

Young adults don't generally carry toffees about. And these were the same kind that my wife used to buy. The taste brought back so many memories. Both of us didn't speak for a minute. I was overwhelmed because I knew she must have brought them especially for me. She shivered again, now warming her nose which had turned light pink and pushing up her spectacles which were resting on the tip of her nose. I smiled and patted her shoulder. After so many years I had found her alone and I didn't know what to say to her. When she was young, she always had something to tell me. But that day she was silent; I was certain that something was wrong.

'Everything all right?' I asked.

'Yes,' she replied without looking at me.

I remembered Shridhar saying she was upset. 'You had a fight with your brother?' I asked.

'No,' she replied.

There was no point hurrying her, so I waited for her to start speaking.

'I was going to go to visit Madhuri Maushi,' she said, 'but I thought it would be better to come and meet you.' After a pause she added, 'Rahul is at home, studying.'

'Yes, I know,' I replied. 'Poor guy.'

She gave me a half-hearted smile and turned away to look at the sunset.

'What's wrong, Janaki? You seem upset.'

'What is wrong is that my brother considers himself to be the most unfortunate person in the world,' she replied in a low voice, still not looking at me.

'Why don't you tell your brother what you feel?' I asked her after a short pause.

'I did,' she replied, looking at her nails. Then, taking a deep breath, she added, 'and the entire family took his side and pounced on me like wild cats pounce on their prey.

'I am sick, sick of all of them,' she said, her eyes moist. 'They just blame everything on reservation. If you don't get admission in college, like Rahul fears he won't; if the bureaucracy doesn't work; if a college doesn't have good teachers—anything and everything! Is something wrong? Whose fault is it? The answer is always: reservation.'

Her eyes were red; she had crossed her arms and was

looking at the sky. But she kept talking in a low, vehement voice. 'Oh! We are very progressive; we don't ask our cook her caste. But will we give up our privileges? Will we ever allow a level playing field? Will we marry someone from another caste or even tolerate such a marriage in our house? Hell, no. Why should we? Our forefathers used religion as an excuse; we use the argument of merit, and we will never allow the caste system to go. Merit is an argument made by those who want to maintain the status quo.

'You see, Ajoba,' she added after a short pause, 'for Rahul, educational institutions are meant to teach the persons who have the most marks. And such a purpose suits his interests, since he's a middle-class, urban, Brahmin boy who has spent his whole life aiming to get good marks. For me, the purpose is social representation. And yet, I get admission, because the system still suits me.'

'Janaki, you are being too hard on yourself,' I said, realizing what she was thinking. 'Just because you are a Brahmin, it doesn't mean that you shouldn't be getting admission anywhere. You worked hard and you deserved…'

'Are you on my side or my brother's?' she said, cutting me off.

'Of course I am on your side. I…'

'You know why I didn't go to Maushi's place?' she interrupted again. 'Because they are all the same. My cousin is in the eleventh standard now and to hear her talk, she might as well give up and die rather than try to get into college in Pune. Her elder sister just got married and moved to America to be with her husband, and she is studying in a private school here. But Maushi still keeps on complaining that she is so unfortunate, they are all so unfortunate… Of course, everyone knows that when she finishes school here, she will also go off to America for further studies. But still, they just won't stop complaining about it being *so* unjust that they should have to face reservation in college admissions. They should be killed, all of them. I just… I can't take them any more. Those self-centred, morally corrupt idiots.'

The sun had set and I could see her in the light of the Diwali lamps that people had started lighting. The street lights would be turned on in a couple of minutes. A few firecrackers could already be heard in the distance. She unwrapped her toffee and placed it in her mouth. When Shridhar came to find us, a few minutes later, she was holding my hand and had placed her head on my shoulder. Life was not going to be easy for her, I feared.

7

I was invited by Shridhar to spend the night at his house on a Sunday a couple of days later—a welcome change from my usual routine. It was the last day of the holidays for everyone. I have always hated the end of the holidays, ever since I was in school, the more so because there are no excuses left to not get back to work.

I was talking with Shridhar who was sitting in his favourite armchair with a shawl wrapped around his shoulders. I could see Anita coming and going from the kitchen and dining area. Anita and Partha were both busy preparing for work the next day. Anita had begun to teach eighth-standard students as well, as the demand for tuitions was rising. Like Rahul's teachers, she had given her tenth-standard students a lot of homework to complete over the holidays and now she would have to check it all. Her days were beginning to become more and more hectic and she was busy preparing for the next week. Janaki would also resume her internship the next day, though she was not at home yet. Rahul, too, had to study hard and attend his tuitions. The mood of the house had changed. Rahul had already shut himself up in his room to study.

After their preparations were over, Partha and Anita joined us in the living room and the conversation was merry and enthusiastic. I was a bit disappointed that Janaki was not present. But then Shridhar reminded me that when she had come to my house, she had told me about her plan to go out for an early dinner with her friends. I had forgotten that part of the conversation completely, but I was cheered knowing that she would return soon.

Janaki hadn't met these friends for a few years, since they had all gone off to their various colleges. Her best friend, Sandhya, was, of course, also going to be a part of the gang. Their get-together was to take place in a restaurant situated in one of the suburbs of Pune, the name of which I, at my age, always forget. But I know that it is at the other end of the city, on the outskirts of Pune. Initially, it was decided that her father would drop her and pick her up. But as both Janaki and Sandhya were going, they managed to convince their parents to allow them to go alone. It's true that at night there is little traffic on the roads. But this fact, instead of making the roads less dangerous to drive on, makes them even more so, as people take the opportunity to see how fast they can go at such times. Janaki's parents, concerned for her safety, had in fact asked her and Sandhya to hire an auto rickshaw instead of going on a two-wheeler. They considered it safer, as the girls would not have to dodge rogue drivers. The girls had agreed, and also promised that they would be back home by eleven o'clock at the latest.

Rahul came out of his room for dinner, looking very tired. He had woken up at five in the morning, had been studying throughout the day almost without a break and was going to have to study well into the night if he wanted to complete his homework. The dinner was a simple one, at my insistence, as I was aware that the family had hosted a huge number of dinners during Diwali and I did not intend to burden either the treasury or their gastro-intestinal systems. As we ate, Shridhar and I reminisced about our childhood Diwalis together, and Anita told us about how she and all her cousins used to visit her grandparents and how much she loved her grandmother's cooking. It became a lively meal, full of laughter, and when Rahul went back to his studies, he seemed a little less tired.

When we returned to the living room to carry on the conversation, I was astonished to see the clock on the wall showing that it was already ten thirty. Janaki was expected to be back in half an hour. As the clock struck ten forty-five, the atmosphere in the house became expectant. Rahul came out of his room shortly afterwards to inquire whether his sister had arrived and decided to sit with us till she came. He sat between his parents who were sitting on the sofa on my left and no one spoke.

Although the lateness of the hour annoyed her parents, they were more worried than angry. Janaki had never been late anywhere. After a little while, Rahul quipped that she would open the door with her key only at eleven p.m. sharp. Her reputation for punctuality had earned her the nickname 'alarm clock' and made her the subject of many jokes within the family. As we laughed, some of the tension dissipated.

At five minutes to eleven, Janaki called her father, saying that the party had just got over. She said that Sandhya was looking for a rickshaw and that they would be home soon. They had been talking to the parents of her other friends who had come to pick them up and it had become late without anyone realizing. She promised that they would not 'hang around' any longer and that they would be home soon.

'She will be home in half an hour,' her parents told each other. 'At least she called.'

'Of course she called! Her reputation was at stake,' Rahul joked.

Partha and Anita were still quite nervous but everyone knew that she would be all right. I know what they were going through. I have felt the same way when one or the other of my sons did not return home on time. And, unlike Janaki, they would never tell me where they were going. We have had quite a lot of fights because of this. Even now, I get worried when they go back to the US after visiting me. They go from Pune to Frankfurt and then take a second flight to New York or San Francisco. I tell them to call me at each leg: first when they reach Frankfurt, next when they reach New York or San Francisco, and third when they reach their own houses. And if their flights are delayed, I want them to inform me about that too. I cannot sleep till I get their third call. My wife also used to sit waiting for the calls with the cordless phone in her hand.

My children never understood why I used to get so upset when they didn't call or called only once instead of all three times. They tried to reassure me that they would be fine. They still try to do that, but now they have realized that I get tense and have accepted it as another of my irritating habits. Or perhaps it is because their own children have started travelling independently that they have greater sympathy for me.

I remember thinking all this while we waited for Janaki. We all looked at each other, at the walls, the ceiling and most importantly, at the clock. Anita had her eyes fixed on it. She had said that she was going to scold Janaki, but I was sure that the first thing that she would do when her daughter entered the house was to hug her. Rahul was also annoyed with his sister for making him feel anxious and preventing him from studying. He had gone back to his bedroom to study after we received her call, only to return after fifteen minutes, saying that he could just not concentrate and might as well wait till his sister came back. The atmosphere had become quite tense. 'But Pune is a safe city,' we all agreed.

Forty-five minutes passed like this. Then the doorbell rang, and Rahul sprang up to open it. But it was Sandhya's parents, who had come to inquire if we had heard anything about the whereabouts of the girls. They had not got a phone call from Sandhya. She had not picked up the phone when they called, almost an hour ago and they had been getting more and more anxious. Partha told them about Janaki's call, and they turned to look at the clock, which was showing a few minutes to midnight.

Sandhya's father, Amit, and Anita both wanted to go and find the girls immediately, but Partha and Sandhya's mother were unsure whether to give them some more time. It would take the girls at least forty-five minutes on the road, and, they reasoned, at night it is sometimes very difficult to find a rickshaw, which would add some more time. While they were uneasily discussing this, Anita had been trying to call both Janaki and Sandhya. As neither of them were answering their mobiles, the parents decided to go out and hunt for them. A further delay was caused because Rahul also wanted to accompany them, but Partha wanted him to stay at home and study. Finally, at half past midnight, just as they were about to get into the car, a very scared Janaki rang her father, begging him in between sobs and disconnected phrases, to come and pick her up.

This time, when Rahul also got into the car, nobody objected. I waited with the family, trying to console Anita and reassure her that whatever had happened, Janaki was safe. Shridhar sat silently at first, with his eyes closed. After some time, he got up and started walking back and forth, looking at the clock and the phone at every turn. It was half past four when a visibly traumatized Janaki came home from the police station.

Court cases can often be traumatic. This is particularly the case if it takes a long time to identify and apprehend the accused. In this case, the first court hearing took place in mid-June 2007. It was November before the stern, grey-haired sessions court judge in his stiff costume gave permission to the prosecution to present their witness. And Janaki stood in the witness box to give testimony in the case of the rape and murder of her best friend, Sandhya.

JANAKI

8

THE PARTY FINISHED LATER THAN I THOUGHT IT WOULD, and the ritual of greeting and chatting with all the parents who had come to pick up their kids delayed us further. I had promised my parents I would be home by eleven, but it was already a quarter to eleven by the time we were done. I knew they'd be worrying, so I told Sandhya to go find a rickshaw while I called and told them about the delay. She would call her parents from the rickshaw.

The restaurant where we had met was down a lane, not on the main road. I stood outside it and tried to call my parents on our landline number, but I could not connect. I saw Sandhya standing on the main road, which was now deserted, waiting for a rickshaw. She waited there for a while, and then decided to walk down the road. Evidently, she had no luck, as she returned and continued down the road in the opposite direction. I decided to call my father's cell phone, hunching over my screen to find his number. When I looked up again, I saw her crossing the main road towards the lane opposite. I was still explaining the reason for the delay, so I didn't pay much attention to what she was doing. I hoped she'd spotted a rickshaw in the dimly-lit lane.

But then, I saw her turn and head back, almost running, in my direction. I knew instinctively that something was wrong. Hastily, I tried to assure Baba that I would be home as soon as possible, to end the call, but even saying that took a few seconds. By then, I could see that somebody was coming

up after Sandhya. I started running towards the mouth of
the lane. As I got closer, I could see that there was indeed
a rickshaw parked in the opposite lane, but now Sandhya
seemed to have vanished. Instead, I heard men's voices
shouting abuses. I could make out the outlines of two men
in the dim light. I suspected that they were drunk. When I
reached the mouth of the lane, I saw a third man, crouching
on the ground.

Then I saw Sandhya. She lay on the ground, struggling
to get up. I saw the third man, the one who was crouching
over her, slap her across her face, once, twice. Then he was
on top of her.

And I stood there, unable to do anything. I could feel
my blood running thick and cold. I could hear my heart
pounding. A shiver went down my spine. I could not move
as I saw him raping her. The men didn't see me as I was still
in the dark, tree-shadowed lane across the road from them.
But had they seen me at that moment, and decided to rape
me as well, I don't think I would have put up a fight. I was
rooted to the spot, unable to think, unable to act, engulfed by
a numbing fear. The fear that every woman carries with her
from childhood onwards; a dread, the anticipation of which
gives us our greatest nightmares. And when the nightmare
comes true, it paralyzes our bodies, making us into statues.

I was released from my paralysis only when I realized that
they were not done with Sandhya. The man had pulled up his
pants and stood, but then one of the other two approached
her. When I realized what was happening, I ran a few steps
instinctively towards my friend, and the man who had just got

up turned. He started walking in my direction. I panicked. I thought he had seen me. I thought he was coming to catch me. I thought they would rape me as well. So, I ran back into the lane.

Only when I reached the other end did I realize that he was not following me. I had been able to see the men only because they were near the streetlights, and they could not have seen me in the darkness. I stood there for a minute, overcome by the relief.

Then I remembered—Sandhya! I had to do something to help her. I tried to pull out my phone to call the police, but my hands were shaking so much that it slipped out of my grasp and fell on the street. I dropped to my hands and knees and desperately felt around for it in the dark. When I finally found it, I simply couldn't remember the helpline number. I tried hard to bring it up, but the only thing I could recollect was the 100 number that I had known since I was a child. I even tried to call that, despite knowing it was futile to dial it from a mobile phone.

Then I had an idea. I ran back to the restaurant where we had met. The shutters were already down, but two waiters were still there. I asked them, begged them for help. They refused. The manager came out while I was talking, but he, too, looked me in the eye and told me that they did not want to get involved, did not want to risk it. He said that the men were most probably members of a local gang and taking 'panga' with them was bad for business. I realized I was wasting time pleading with them; that he simply didn't care about Sandhya or me. Finally, I asked them to at least give me the police's helpline number. Again and again, I called. No use. One helpline number did not function and the other simply rang endlessly. By the time I gave up, the waiters had all disappeared.

I ran onwards, hoping to find another shop or perhaps a car—someone I could ask for help. But not a single vehicle drove by and there was nobody on the road. The area was full of small shops, restaurants and offices, all with their shutters drawn and not a single window lit from within. But when I stopped, breathless, I saw a medical shop which was open, with a group of young men sitting outside. They were playing cards and chatting loudly, probably drunk. One of them must have been the night attendant at the shop. I could ask them for help.

I started to walk up to them, but a thought made me freeze in my tracks. 'What if they do the same to you as the others are doing to Sandhya?' a voice said inside my head. I turned and started running away. They either didn't see me or chose to ignore me, much to my relief. But as I ran, again I remembered—Sandhya. I turned back towards the men, but again, as I approached my fears returned, and I didn't have the courage to go closer to them. In the end, I did not ask them for help.

As I walked back towards where I had left Sandhya, I saw from a distance that the men were hurriedly getting inside the rickshaw. It sped away, leaving Sandhya lying on the footpath. In that moment, I felt relief, that with their departure, the ordeal was over, truly over.

When I got closer, I realized that what I had witnessed

was only a small part of what had happened. Sandhya had not only been gang-raped but had also been stabbed in the stomach. I remember sitting there on the pavement with her head in my lap, trying to revive her, crying and begging her to speak. When I finally came to my senses, some time later, a minute or maybe twenty, I called for an ambulance. Then, as I waited for the ambulance, I remembered to call my father. I should have called him earlier for help. It just hadn't occurred to me.

Surprisingly, the ambulance reached us before my father did. I sat in it but I don't remember anything about the journey. I did not pray. I did not ask the paramedics if she would live. I didn't ask them to save her life. I just sat there, in shock. For the entire time that it took us to reach the nearest hospital, I was devoid of all thought.

Sandhya was declared dead on arrival. She had been stabbed brutally a number of times. The doctor told me that her small intestine had been badly damaged. Her left gastric artery, one of the arteries that supplies blood to the stomach, had been ruptured. Too much blood had already been lost before we reached the hospital. I could not understand what the doctor was saying then. I just nodded.

When my father and the others reached the restaurant and they didn't find Sandhya or I there, they got worried. I hadn't let them know that we—or rather, Sandhya's body and I—were at the hospital. He called me repeatedly, but I didn't realize that the phone was ringing. Was it shock? Was it simply that I was busy talking to the police officers who had come to the hospital? I don't know. I just didn't hear it. The rest is a blur, like in a nightmare where you have no control over your actions; all that I did then was involuntary.

Amit Uncle also tried to call Sandhya, but her phone was in her purse which had been left on the pavement. Only when they found the purse did they begin to suspect that something was seriously wrong. They were about to call the police when I returned from the hospital in a police van, to show the constables the 'crime scene'.

When I saw my father, I stood there, stunned. I looked at him and then at Rahul, feeling dazed at their normal, concerned, kindly presence. Then I saw Amit Uncle. I couldn't look at him. He knew. He knew immediately. The police said something to him. He was taken to the hospital. I think my father called my mother to tell her what had happened, but I am not sure.

I remember being taken to the police station after that, and being told to make a statement on the record about what had happened. Rahul sat next to me and held my hand, throughout; it was his presence that prevented me from collapsing. I started narrating the whole story. I told them how I saw her running from a distance. I told them how I ran to the mouth of the road, only to see her being raped. I told them how I had tried to get help, but couldn't find any. I told them how I saw the men fleeing the spot later, leaving my friend's body on the road. I did not realize that I was speaking very fast, almost without taking a breath. The police officer who was writing this down tried to stop me a couple of times to ask me something, but I ignored him and continued talking. I needed to talk, to tell everything that had happened. As I spoke, I could feel Rahul's grip on my hand getting tighter and tighter, and after some time, he also draped his arm around my shoulders. That is what kept me going until they told me that an FIR had been filed against unidentified persons and to come again to describe the three men so that the artists could prepare their sketches.

While Rahul and I were in the police station, my father had gone back home and brought Sandhya's mother to the hospital, to be with Amit Uncle. When it was time for us to leave, Rahul guided me back to the car and sat next to me. It was half-past four in the morning when I reached home. I went straight to my bedroom. I didn't have the emotional strength to stand anymore. I wanted to sleep and get away from the world as much as possible. My grandfather gave me sleeping pills, but sleep eluded me that day. And ever since, it has eluded me many times.

9

AT SANDHYA'S CREMATION, IT WAS COLD. I WAS WEARING the pink jacket she had given me. I looked at my hands and placed them on my stomach. I was unhurt, but my childhood friend was now going to be nothing but ashes. I finally had to face the fact that I would never see her again. Sandhya was gone forever. I didn't want to watch the flames consume her. As if averting my eyes was going to change the reality. The truth is that I did not want to accept that she was gone, that I would never hear her voice again. I made myself look at the pyre, the flames, the huge logs and heaps of flowers, with Sandhya in there, somewhere. Tears flooded my eyes and I tried to gulp them down. I bowed my head and closed my eyes.

When the ceremony was over, I tried to leave hurriedly. But I had to go past Sandhya's mother. She was weeping quietly into her handkerchief and I didn't want to face her. What would I tell her? What excuse could I give her for being unhurt and alive while her daughter was gone forever? How could I meet her eyes? And what would I see in them? Hate? Contempt? Regret that it was not me on the pyre? Or just sorrow, unbearable sorrow? I did not dare to look at her. I bowed my head and tried to go past quietly. But she caught up with me. She hugged me and cried, resting her head on my shoulder. I involuntarily stroked her back and held her close. Then she patted my shoulder without looking at me. She turned and walked away with the aid of her husband.

And I kept standing there, staring at their backs, my vision blurred.

A month after Sandhya's death, I met them at the police station. My mother and father had been going to their house almost every day, trying to console them as much as possible. But I'd tried to avoid them. I knew by now that they did not blame me for their daughter's death, but still, I felt unable to meet their eyes. I just could not bear to see their terrible suffering, all their emotions on the surface, like an open wound. But when my parents told me that Uncle and Aunty were going to go to the police station to find out whether they had found the men who murdered my friend, I felt that I had to be there also. I wanted to know what was happening, I needed to know if those men had been caught.

We were told that it was a matter of time. The police had no names, no suspects. When we tried to ask them about the details of the investigation, we were shunted out of the police station. But the police became very accommodating later, after they got a call from 'above'. In the end, the investigating officer met us and promised that he would ensure prompt action. We decided to wait for some time to see if he intended to keep his promise. He did, and three months after the night at the restaurant, the three rapists were identified. Three months after that, they were arrested in Mumbai.

Every person accused of a crime has certain rights, which are protected to ensure that both they and the victims receive justice. But in reality, justice is usually not served, due to the delays which have unfortunately become a characteristic of our judicial system Eight years have passed since then, and the trial is still continuing, now, in 2014. Even today, when we inquire, we are told that not much time has been wasted, that progress in this case is faster than in most other cases. And what is worse is that this may well be true.

We came to know about the backgrounds of all three men from the police records and from the evidence presented in court. Their confessions, though inadmissible in court as they were made to the police and therefore possibly extorted with violence, were disclosed to us. From this, and with what I had myself witnessed, I learnt about the basic facts around Sandhya's rape.

Raghav and Mohammed Ali were both rickshaw drivers in their mid twenties. Mohan was Raghav's cousin, seventeen years old and therefore a juvenile for the purposes of the court. He had dropped out of school in the ninth standard and used to do small jobs: cleaning tables in restaurants, a short stint as a newspaper delivery boy, etc. But at that time, he was unemployed. He used to spend a lot of time with his cousin Raghav, and had started stealing money from home for alcohol. When his parents found out that he was on his way to becoming an alcoholic, they kicked him out of the house. Raghav's mother allowed him to live with her (her husband had passed away a couple of years before). Raghav had a younger sister who was going to be married. Usually he used to drive the rickshaw during the day, but he had started driving at night to earn more money for his sister's wedding.

Unlike Raghav and Mohan, Mohammad Ali was not from

Pune. He was from a village in Uttar Pradesh and had a wife and parents there. The police later told us that they had traced his family at the time of their initial investigation but, as the family had not had any contact with Mohammad Ali, they hadn't mentioned it to us. The family had stopped hearing from him all of a sudden. They had also stopped receiving the money he used to send home every month. The police figured out that he had not been in contact with them since around the time of the rape.

Mohammed Ali had come to Mumbai six years ago, like many people before and after him, to find a job. The city is crowded with such people from different parts of the country. Every person thinks that he is the next Dhirubhai Ambani, but only a few lucky, skilled and intelligent ones manage to script their own rags-to-riches story. The city swallows the rest, crushing their dreams.

Mumbai is the city of opportunities. It works like a machine, each component of which is a human being, running hard to reach somewhere, to achieve something, to fulfil their dreams. But no one knows what they are running for. Mohammed Ali was one of the people who came to Mumbai with a dream, but he soon realized that Mumbai was not what he thought it would be. He did some small jobs, but spent the little money that he could make on survival. He did not even earn enough money to send home. A man from his village had settled down in Pune, and he suggested that Mohammed Ali should move there. At first, Mohammed Ali worked in his shop and lived in his house. Then he was introduced to someone who owned two rickshaws, and began to regularly drive one of them.

Raghav and Mohammed Ali were the same age and lived in the same area. They were both rickshaw drivers. They bought alcohol at the same shop and smoked bidis at the same stall. They became friends. Poverty united them and religion, place of birth and mother tongue all failed to divide them. When Raghav started driving at night, Mohammed Ali used to come and give him company. Soon, Mohan also joined them. They started drinking. In the beginning, Raghav used to try to find as many customers as possible. But later, he began to wait till midnight, take only a few customers, and charge higher rates.

That night, they had been drinking since nine o'clock. When Sandhya came to hire a rickshaw it was eleven. They said that she had crossed the road towards them, but when she saw that they were drunk, she had turned back. They said that they had gotten very angry and had felt insulted by the arrogance of this 'city girl'. That is why they had raped her. The man who I had seen raping Sandhya first was Raghav. Then Mohammed Ali raped her. And then Mohan raped her. After they were done, they broke the bottle from which they had been drinking and cut her with the glass pieces. They continued doing this even after she became unconscious. Only then did they realize that they had committed a crime and would have to go to jail. They panicked. They thought that Sandhya would be able to recognize them and testify against them. So, they decided to remove that possibility, by killing her. First, Raghav used his knife to stab her, followed by Mohammed Ali, and then Mohan. Once they were sure she was dead, they got into the rickshaw and fled.

They went back to their homes that night. From the next

day, they stopped going out to work. They had read in the newspapers that the police can track mobile phones, so they switched theirs off. After a few days, when Raghav's mother started asking questions, they thought it was time to flee. Mohammed Ali suggested going to Mumbai and they left their homes overnight. They said they thought they could lose themselves in the crowds of the big city. They lived there for six months, keeping a low profile. Then one day, believing that the police would not be looking for them anymore, Raghav called his mother to inform her that he was okay. The next thing they knew, the police had arrested them.

Before the trial began, I was helped by the support of my friends and teachers at the law college. Although it did not grab as much media attention as cases of rape have recently been getting, the gruesomeness of the crime, coupled with the fact that one of their own was actually involved, really shook them up. The papers moved on to newer and equally horrifying news, but my friends, even unexpected ones, like Pratiksha, stayed with me as long as I needed them. The advice of my teachers proved valuable in understanding the processes through which the judiciary operates. They were the ones who first warned me that Raghav and Mohammed Ali might plead 'not guilty' when the trial began—which turned out to be the case.

In the end, at least we knew that the three men had been arrested. When the trial began in June 2007, we had some hope that justice would follow, which gave us a little peace of mind. But this peace of mind did not last for long.

10

WHY DID I INVITE AJOBA TO LIVE WITH ME? WAS IT because I knew that he would let me live my life? Someone who would not try to suffocate me, but at the same time, be there to support me if I needed help? The only other person I know who would have been equally willing to support my need for independence was Pratiksha. But I had distanced myself from her. I had reached a point where I had no tolerance left. I couldn't even tolerate help.

I do miss her now. Perhaps if I try to contact her she might forgive me. She did once before.

I met Pratiksha when I was studying for my BA. Sandhya had chosen commerce after we left school, and Pratiksha filled the gap she left in my life. We met for the first time while taking admission in the college. Later, two other girls joined our group: Priyanka and Neha. But over time, Pratiksha and I became good friends because we saw things in much the same way.

One rainy July day, the four of us were sitting in the canteen. Strong winds were howling outside, so the atmosphere was gloomy and everybody was bored. Along with Pratiksha, I tried to start a conversation.

'I hate this rain,' she said. 'It's so boring. We can't do anything.'

'It's not all that bad,' I said. 'It'll get over in a few days.

When it's hot we keep wanting the rains and now we are already bored.'

'What can we do? We just have to sit indoors and it's irritating. I'm so pissed,' Neha replied.

'Then why don't we go out and have some fun?' I said. 'Let's go to Lonavala this Sunday.'

The idea of going to the hill station immediately put a smile on Neha's face.

'But I have to attend my cousin's wedding this Sunday,' objected Priyanka. 'We'll have to postpone the plan.'

Neha rolled her eyes at this obstacle, but she was clearly disappointed. Pratiksha and I were disappointed as well. But Priyanka was over the moon about this wedding, and eagerly looking forward to wearing the new clothes and jewelry that she and her mother had bought especially for the occasion. She had also been dropping subtle hints that she might herself be 'seen' for marriage there. Her father had even said that she should tell him if she saw anyone interesting, so that he could make inquiries about whether the person she liked was 'eligible'. What followed was the usual discussion about marriages and weddings. Both Priyanka and Neha badly wanted to get married soon, and were always fascinated by the details of weddings. I have always felt this obsession with marriage, which almost always borders on irrationality, to be extremely irritating. I've never understood why the subject of marriage makes many otherwise rational and intelligent women act as if that is the final and ultimate aim of their lives, instead of being only an aspect—albeit an important one. And so I took no part in it.

The attitude of girls like Priyanka and Neha still perplexes me, but in those days, it used to enrage me, so I did not notice that Pratiksha was also sitting mutely. I had just started making new friends and I didn't want a fight, so I silently listened to them going on and on about how perfect they wanted their weddings to be. But when Neha said that she was waiting eagerly to get married so that she could use the honorific term usually reserved for husbands, it became too much for me to bear.

So I stated my views, although in very mild language. I tried to dispel their notions that life after marriage is all hunky dory, but to no avail. I tried to bring to their notice that, for women, historically, and even today, exploitation and violence have often accompanied marriage as an institution. When I gave examples of practices like sati and keshvapan, I received the expected response that 'such things don't happen anymore these days'. When I spoke about violence for the sake of dowry, I got justifications blaming the patriarchal social structure, but not acknowledging that marriage is often used to reinforce that very same patriarchal structure. What I had not expected was the support that I received from Pratiksha. She was not only on my side, but she also spoke out strongly. We both said that we found this glorification of marriage to be illogical and infuriating. Further, we both also thought that we didn't need to be seriously considering the matter of marriage anyway and should be concentrating our energies elsewhere. While we both agreed that happy marriages do exist, we said that one has to be extremely cautious while making decisions about whether to marry, when and to whom.

In the end, a clearly exasperated Priyanka said, 'You guys think too much. This way you will never get married.'

'Great,' we replied, which ended the conversation.

But I realized that I had an ally.

Pratiksha and I were great friends by the time we finished our BA. I was keen to join a law college, despite my family's opposition to the profession, and I was delighted when she joined the same college. Other than Sandhya, she was the one friend I could confide in.

In the first semester, we had a subject called Laws relating to Women and Children. There was also a gender studies cell in our college which was quite active. They ran awareness campaigns and offered legal aid to women in distress. Naturally, both of us joined this cell. But, as the second semester began, my interest in the activities of the cell began to dwindle. The subjects we learned in college changed. The laws related to women were no longer a part of our coursework. Some discussions which took place in the cell also turned me off.

One incident in particular troubled me. As part of the gender studies cell, we had invited a lawyer (female, of course), who worked with an NGO that provided aid to victims of domestic violence. After her speech, everyone, including Pratiksha, was very touched by her stories. I was also not totally unaffected. But I was the only one to notice that she did not elaborate upon the application of the law in her stories. And perhaps because of this, none of the questions that the audience asked were related to the law, except mine.

I tried to raise this point with Pratiksha after her enthusiasm for the speaker calmed down a bit. 'She spoke quite well, Pratiksha,' I said. 'But I had thought that she would talk a bit more about the law. I mean, she is a lawyer. She is socially committed, no doubt. But I don't really think she is a good lawyer.'

'Of course she must be a good lawyer,' Pratiksha replied. 'She is not like the others who defend murderers. She is fighting for an important cause.'

'Yes, the cause is important,' I agreed. 'But don't you see that she is not really bothered about how good she is at understanding the law? She couldn't answer any of my questions. We are law students, Pratiksha; we cannot have the same attitude as her. We must understand the importance of excellence. I want to master the skills required to be a good lawyer. Isn't that equally important? As women, we must strive to be good in our fields, whatever that field maybe. We must first become good lawyers or doctors or nurses or clerks. Commitment to a cause is just a part of it...'

'You are evading the issue, Janaki,' she said, cutting me off. 'She was speaking about an important topic. A topic that most of your so-called good lawyers don't talk about. They talk only about the law, without caring about anything else. And she must be good at law also. Only because she cannot speak in fluent English...'

'This has nothing to do with her ability to speak English,' I interjected. 'She could have answered me in Marathi or Hindi. She spoke half the time in Hindi anyway. But still she did not answer any of my questions.'

'Oh! Stop being so snobbish, Janaki. She was amazing,' Pratiksha replied.

The conversation ended there, but after this, I gradually stopped attending the activities of the cell.

Pratiksha continued to be a keen participant. At first, she did not mention my lack of interest, but after a couple of weeks, she asked me about it. I made excuses, saying that I had been busy. But when I still did not appear at meetings, she tried to pressure me into coming with her. I was getting tired of her nagging. Matters came to a head when she confronted me just after a class.

'Where were you?' she asked angrily, coming up to me. 'You promised you'd come. Don't say you're busy.'

'I'm bored of all this feminist chatter,' I said, equally angry.

She was startled. As she struggled for words, I continued relentlessly.

'I have come to resent your self-righteous attitude. I...'

'You're calling me self-righteous? And what about you, Janaki? What about...'

'I just don't want to go on with this any more, okay?' I said, cutting her off. 'Only because I'm a woman, you think I have to become an activist and fight for women's rights...'

'But you believe in what we are saying. What has happened to you all of a sudden?' she asked, biting her lip.

'It's not "all of a sudden." I've been trying to explain this to you for a long time. I want to be a lawyer. A good lawyer. Do you remember the discussion we had when that lady from the NGO came to talk to us? Do you remember what I said to you then?' I continued my original argument. 'Why do I have to do all this? Why are you forcing me? If I had been a guy you wouldn't have made me do this. You wouldn't…'

'Oh stop it, Janaki. No one is forcing you,' she said, cutting me off. 'There are plenty of girls inside and outside this college who, like you, are "not interested". I only asked because I thought you cared. Sorry I asked. I judged you wrongly. I thought that you had the sensitivity and the guts to fight.'

'I am fighting at my personal level. Why do I have to fight for everyone?'

'Because if we don't, who will? Only the women who are being exploited? And tomorrow, if you are in that position, what will you do? Will there be anyone to support you then? This affects us all, Janaki. I am not stopping you from becoming a lawyer. I am not saying that as a lawyer you should take up only cases of women. Don't take up even a single case related to women if you want. But there is more than enough reason for you to care,' she replied.

I paused, thinking about her words. But my doubts weren't allayed. 'Feminism is a bottomless well, Pratiksha. If I enter it I'll never get out. I'll never be happy,' I said at last.

'And outside, you'll be happy, do you think?' she asked bitterly. 'And being happy is all that matters to you, does it?'

'I care, Pratiksha! I do,' I defended myself. 'But I don't want to pledge my life to this. There are many things that are wrong in our society, Pratiksha. You've got so drawn into this that you don't see anything else. You've become blind. You don't see poverty, you don't see casteism. Feminism means equality; right? But you don't seem to recognize exploitation on any grounds other than gender.'

After a pause she replied, 'Okay. So you think we are idiots fighting without a cause. And all this is a farce we have put up only to take away attention from the "real", "important" issues. Thanks for letting me know your opinion about us. Next time when I meet an abused woman, I'll tell her that her problems aren't real. I won't ask you again why you don't come with us. You can go, I won't stop you. You don't have to talk to me ever again.' And she left.

I tried to talk to her after a couple of days but she avoided me. I regretted every word I had said. But there was no way to explain to her why I was no longer interested. I thought that I had lost her and she would never speak to me again. But she forgave me and was there for me when I needed her. Then, again, I made her leave me. And we have never spoken since.

11

Pratiksha and I had not spoken for more than a year by the time of Sandhya's murder. I did not attend lectures for a week, and when I finally went to college, I told my friends that I wanted to be left alone. After the lectures finished on my first day back, I was sitting alone at my desk. That's when Pratiksha came and sat next to me. She knew that I didn't need condolences. I didn't need someone to tell me that everything would be all right. I needed someone who would listen to me. Someone whom I could show my anger to. And, perhaps, someone who would understand when I blamed myself for Sandhya's rape … and who would also tell me that it was not my fault.

Ironic as it may sound, I received support from the same gender studies cell which I had disapproved of and left. Pratiksha took me to the teachers involved with the cell and they gave me both advice and encouragement. She also came with me to court on the day I was to give testimony. I think that it was her presence, along with Rahul's and Ajoba's, that stopped me from breaking down during the cross-examination. I had been warned by the teachers in advance about how aggressive defence lawyers can be, which helped me to prepare a bit. But nothing could prepare me enough for what was in store for me that day.

After that ordeal was over, Pratiksha spent some time with me and tried to calm me down. The next day, she again took me to meet the teachers, who continued to be supportive.

As the days passed, I started spending more and more time with Pratiksha. When I started attending the activities of the cell again, I thought back to my reasons for leaving it in the first place, but I decided to ignore them, as I badly needed help. I was expected to attend all the meetings of the cell and contribute to every discussion. I was called on to narrate my experience countless times. Many of the members of the cell met me after the sessions and even beforehand, to offer their condolences. In the beginning, it helped. But slowly, my relationship with the rest of the members started becoming uncomfortable. I grew tired of their sympathy, tired of the other women that they listed as examples, tired of being part of a list of victims. It was as if they did not want me to move on and live the rest of my life.

As I was asked to recount my experiences repeatedly, I slowly started becoming hostile towards them. In addition to asking me to narrate the incident, they also started asking me questions about the factual details. They wanted me to remember every detail of my ordeal and to speak about it again and again. I had already been cross-examined once by the defence counsel and was in no state to be interrogated by them. I felt as though I was being made a culprit and a victim at the same time. And I didn't want to be a victim any more. I wanted to live.

I cut my ties with the cell and fought with Pratiksha once more. I blamed her for making me a victim. I said that the only reason that she had helped me was because she wanted to pity me. I accused her, quite unjustly, of helping me only for revenge for how I'd criticized her earlier. I told her that I didn't want her help. We haven't spoken since.

AJOBA

12

AFTER PARTHA, RAHUL AND AMIT LEFT, WE TRIED TO wait patiently, but the tension continued to thicken in the room. When the phone rang, all of us jumped, and Anita nearly shrieked. It was Partha, calling from the police station. All three of us were dumbstruck; I felt almost unable to comprehend what he was saying. He told us that Janaki was talking to the police officers, telling them about Sandhya. I could see Sandhya in my mind's eye, her dark oval eyes, her long nose. The same Sandhya with whom Janaki had shared her anguish when the teacher had reprimanded her. When they were young they had been inseparable, running from one house to the other, playing. Even as they grew up and choose different courses as students they had remained very close. I remembered her sweet smile. 'The smile is gone,' I said to myself, 'gone forever.' I didn't want to imagine what must have happened to her.

Anita put the phone down and sat unmoving for some time. Shridhar and I both kept silent; I, at least, was unable to say anything. Then the doorbell rang—Sandhya's mother. She had just heard the news from Amit and was preparing to go to the hospital. She looked dazed, but spoke animatedly, in a high tone, while incessantly fidgeting with her fingers. She was unable to sit in one place and kept repeating that she had to go to the hospital. Anita had already called Partha and asked him to come to take them there. Each time that Sandhya's mother said that she had to go to the hospital, Anita would ask her to wait till Partha came to pick them up, and she would sit down again, mutely. But again, after a couple of minutes, she would get up and say that she had to go to the hospital. Anita tried to talk to her, telling her that Partha was on his way, but I felt unable to join in the attempt to distract her mind from the horrors it must have been relentlessly playing. I felt that I was an outsider for Sandhya's family, and I didn't want to impose.

I wanted to talk to Janaki, meet her. When Partha returned, I had hoped that Janaki would come back with him. But she was still at the police station, recording her statement, with only Rahul for company. It was half-past four when she finally returned. She was not crying, but her face was unrecognizable. I don't think that she was even able to see properly. Rahul was supporting her, holding her arm. He was crying.

Janaki went into her room with her brother. Her mother and father both followed her. After a few minutes, Partha came out and headed back to the hospital. Some time later, Anita, too, came out. 'She is not speaking,' she said, biting her lip, distressed. 'She is not even crying. She said she wants to be left alone.'

Shridhar had been sitting on his chair with his eyes closed. He got up and went inside to Janaki. He sat with her for some time as well, but when he came out, he said he was prescribing her a sleeping pill. I had been sitting next to Anita on the sofa, holding her hand. Shridhar patted her shoulder, telling her to try to get some sleep herself, as he went to his bedroom.

I went into Janaki's room. She was lying on her side, with her back against the wall, legs drawn close to her chest and her arms wrapped around them in a tight embrace. Her eyes were closed, but she was facing Rahul's bed, exactly opposite. Rahul was sitting on the floor between the two beds, with his forehead on Janaki's bed in front of her knees. He was holding her, his hand gripping her upper arm. When I went in, he looked up and saw me. Then he got up and hugged me and I patted him on the back. He sat back down on his own bed.

I went and sat next to Janaki on her bed. She had opened her eyes when I'd come in, but continued to stare at nothing, dully, with no expression on her face. I touched her hair gently, and she turned the same abstracted gaze to me.

'What happened is not your fault. You are not responsible for this,' I said.

For a minute she stared at me. Then she turned her whole body towards the wall and started to cry

13

LATER THAT WEEK, THE POLICE ARTISTS PUT UP POSTERS of the wanted men, based on Janaki's descriptions, in the area around the restaurant. The local restaurant and shop owners were questioned, as were the waiters and the manager to whom Janaki had appealed for help. Their statements were recorded. All of this took several days. Janaki had not been able to note down the registration number of the rickshaw. The police, however, assured us that this would not be a major impediment to the search.

By the end of the week, the post-mortem report was prepared. It confirmed that Sandhya had been violently raped. She had been more severely injured than any of us had realized. The report showed that the vaginal tissue was severely injured and she had suffered major internal bleeding. Pieces of glass were found inside her vagina. The police had found broken glass bottles at the crime scene which confirmed Janaki's statements that the accused seemed to have been drinking. Tests later confirmed that the glass found inside Sandhya was from the same glass bottles. I could not believe the depths of barbarity to which people can sink. I don't want to even imagine what her parents would have felt at realizing the pain that Sandhya had suffered. I was with Janaki when we heard about the report's contents. Her face betrayed her agony, but she refused to talk about it, even to her brother or me.

After all the evidence was collected, Sandhya's body

was finally handed over to her parents. I did not go to the cremation. I may have become almost a part of Janaki's family, but for Sandhya's parents, I was still an outsider. I think they deserved some privacy. But, as a father myself, I can imagine how they must have felt when seeing their daughter's body being turned to ash; how ardently they must have wished that they were in her place. Sandhya was their only child.

The police had reassured us that the culprits would be caught as soon as possible, but eight years have passed since the death of their daughter and Sandhya has still not got justice. They have tried their hardest to further the progress of the case, but at some level, they still cannot believe that she is gone.

The police investigation started. For the first week or so, they were constantly around, making many inquiries, both around the restaurant and at Shridhar's house, cross-checking parts of Janaki's statement. But then the investigation cooled down. At first, when Sandhya's parents or Janaki tried to get information about the progress of the investigation, the police would respond. But after some time, they were politely brushed off. If they had been poor, they would have been thrown out of the police station. They were not poor, so they were politely escorted out, with a litany of platitudes. The police have other duties to perform too, you know. And when has justice for women, their safety or their security been a priority for our society, or for the police, who, in the end, are a part of the same society?

Janaki started going to the police station after college to make inquiries. I started accompanying her as well. If it ever happened that Janaki was unable to come, then I would go with Sandhya's parents because they went every day, without fail. Two months passed by, but the rapists had not even been identified and named. That was the first glimpse that I had of the delays in our police and judicial systems.

Finally, we decided that something had to be done. That was when I realized how delays can be reduced if you belong to a particular class; how our police can adopt different approaches for different persons. Amit was a doctor and, of course, had some political contacts. He reached out to the MP of his constituency and was taken seriously because he was respected and had some influence in the community. Within a few days, the investigating officer politely requested Sandhya's parents to come to the police station and reassured them that the police were trying their best to find the culprits. The MP had called on their behalf.

The rickshaw was never traced. In the end, the police used mobile phone records to find the three men. The restaurant was not in a residential area, and most of the other establishments there had shut by the time Sandhya had gone looking for the rickshaw. Thus, there were very few cell phones in that area at that time. A list of all cell phone owners who were present there was drawn up based on the call records, and they were called to the police station. Five youngsters were detained and questioned. One of them was a medical shop attendant and the rest claimed that they had been with the attendant that night. Based on their own observations and Janaki's testimony about seeing a group of men outside a medical shop that night, the police concluded that they were innocent, but insisted on verifying this with forensic evidence. Those results showed that they were not the men who had raped Sandhya, and they were allowed to go.

Apart from this set, there were three more numbers in the list that were listed as belonging to young men. All three of them were switched off, which led the police to believe that they belonged to the culprits. The posters based on Janaki's descriptions were shown to rickshaw drivers in the area, who confirmed that the suspects were the same persons named in the mobile companies' records. Finally, the rapists were identified. Their names were Raghav, Mohan and Mohammed Ali.

After this breakthrough, the investigation continued, but for some time, the police could make no headway. The mobiles continued to be switched off and untraceable. The police found out that Raghav and Mohan were cousins and questioned their families, but they had no idea about the whereabouts of their sons. Mohammed Ali was not from Pune and no one seemed to have any information about him either. Six months later, by end of April 2007, the police were no closer to nabbing the suspects. They seemed to have disappeared.

Then, in May, they made one mistake. Raghav, believing that the surveillance must have stopped, switched on his cell phone to call his mother in Pune and then switched it off again. The police were alerted that he, at least, had fled to Mumbai. The investigating team went there, and were soon able to catch all three suspects. They were brought back to Pune to be tried.

We were told by the police about the arrest and detention. Raghav and Mohammed Ali were sent to police custody. Mohan was seventeen at the time of the rape, as attested by his school records, so he was sent to an observation home for juveniles.

In custody, Raghav and Mohammed Ali confessed. They told the police exactly what had happened and the police passed the information on to us. Vaginal swabs had been taken at the time of the post-mortem, and DNA tests conducted on the three proved that they had been the rapists.

But one major problem that the investigators faced was that the knife used to stab Sandhya was never recovered. The DNA reports would show irrefutably that the men had raped Sandhya. But in order to build a rock-solid case against the men and prove that they had also killed her, recovering the knife was necessary. If the knife was not found, we would have to rely completely on circumstantial evidence and they could claim that even if they had raped her, they had not killed her, to get a less severe sentence.

According to the police, Raghav had said during the interrogation that he had thrown the knife into a dustbin nearby, while they were escaping in the auto rickshaw. The police told us that they had searched the area more than once when they first began the investigation, but I suspect that they had not done their work properly. Their handling of the forensic evidence had been shoddy, to say the least. They had preserved the vaginal swabs only after we had applied to them to do so. Raghav might also have disposed of the knife in some other way and may have lied to the police to protect himself.

A legal-aid lawyer was appointed by the court to defend the three men as they did not have a lawyer of their own, and probably would not have been able to afford to pay one. We had expected that the accused would plead 'guilty', as they had confessed to the police. But by the time the trial began in mid-June, their lawyer had persuaded them to plead 'not guilty'. In court, they claimed that they had been pressured by the police to confess. Confessions made in police custody are not treated as evidence.

As the trial began, Janaki became more and more withdrawn. She did not speak openly to anyone anymore. She stopped talking to her parents almost completely. She stopped going out with her friends and locked herself in her bedroom. She had lost weight. She continued to go to college, but there was an emptiness about her which was depressing. Looking at her face, it seemed inconceivable that a smile could have ever appeared on it. She went back and forth between the police station and the court as though she had made it her mission to get justice for her friend.

14

In June 2007, Mohan, the juvenile, was presented before the Juvenile Justice Board, while the other two stood trial in court. The police presented all the physical evidence collected by them in court, including the mobile phones, the broken glass bottle, the mobile phone records, etc. Forensic reports were also presented in court, including the three suspects' fingerprints on the glass bottles. The same evidence was also presented before the Juvenile Justice Board.

It was November when Janaki was summoned to give her testimony. Her parents, Rahul and I had gone to the court to give Janaki moral support. Sandhya's parents were also present, and one of Janaki's friends from college had also turned up. I don't remember her name.

The public prosecutor was about forty-five years old, clean shaven with obviously dyed hair and round spectacles. He had a plump nose on the lower edge of which rested his round gold spectacles. He habitually furrowed his brow and interlinked his fingers when he spoke, usually in a low and firm voice. His face usually had a serious expression, enhancing his air of importance. He was a rather busy man, so he had met Janaki only once, and that too very briefly, before the examination began. I was present during this meeting. He told us that her testimony would be crucial in proving that Sandhya's death was caused by the accused men, as the murder weapon had never been found. 'There is no forensic evidence to prove that they killed your friend. Therefore,' he told Janaki, 'you must remember what you saw, and tell that clearly in court.' By then, a year had passed since that night, so the prosecutor told her to refresh her memory and be ready to tell the court every detail. He also cautioned her to avoid any discrepancy in her statements.

The public prosecutor began the examination for the court. He asked Janaki to recount what had happened, in minute detail. While she was going through her narration, he interrupted her a couple of times to ask questions. In the end, he asked her if she was sure that the accused were the people whom she had seen that night, and she said she was. Then he asked her if she had seen them stabbing Sandhya, to which she replied in the negative, but added that she had seen them running from the spot. Then he asked her if she was the person who had called the ambulance and she again replied that she was. Then he thanked her and the examination was over.

The defence lawyer was of about the same age as the public prosecutor, but with a sprinkling of grey hair. He had big eyes which reminded me of an owl, and very bushy eyebrows, as well as a neatly trimmed beard. His spectacles dangled on a string, and usually rested on his chest. He looked very serious as he stood up to cross-examine Janaki. The outcome of the murder charge rested heavily on her testimony and it was his job to shake it.

'The victim was your close friend?' he asked in a low and emotionless voice.

'Yes,' replied Janaki calmly.

'You said that you saw her being raped by the accused?'

'Yes,' she replied again.

'But you did not see them stabbing her?' he asked.

'No, I did not,' she replied. I could see that she was making an effort to remain as calm as possible.

'When you saw the accused coming up behind your friend, did you try to alert her? Did you ask her to flee?' he asked, looking at her seriously.

'No. There was no time and Sandhya was too far from me... I was talking on the phone,' she replied, looking at her lap.

'Did you try to help her?' he asked.

'I was alone. They would have raped me as well. I tried to get help but there was nobody around. And the waiters whom I asked for help would not help me. Nobody was ready to help me,' she replied in a soft voice.

'But you didn't call the police,' he questioned, continuing to stare at her.

'I did. I tried to call, but at first I couldn't remember the number. Later, I got the helpline numbers from the waiters, but they were not functioning,' Janaki responded. She sounded and looked tired already. I hoped that she would not burst out crying during the cross-examination.

'You said you were standing on the other side of the road behind a tree, right?' he continued.

'Yes,' she replied. The strength in her voice made me realize that she had recovered, at least for the time being. 'Yes, I stood behind the tree and saw him (here she pointed at Raghav) raping Sandhya. Then I ran for help because I saw that he (here she pointed at Mohammed Ali) was going to rape her as well,' she added.

'Why didn't you run immediately?' he asked.

'I…I was not sure what was happening. I…' she said, stammering a bit. 'I was so shocked that…that…'

'So you were in a state of shock when you saw this,' the defence lawyer said.

'I was not "in shock". I was shocked, but I was quite alert and my memory was not affected by this,' she hit back.

The defence lawyer ignored her retort. 'Your Honour, the witness has just stated that she was in a state of shock after seeing her friend being raped. This fact should be noted,' he said, addressing the judge.

He turned back to Janaki. 'Is it possible that because you were in shock you really didn't see the persons who were raping your friend? Because psychologists say that shock can affect memory,' he said, his voice sounding concerned.

'No, I remember that these men raped my friend.' Though calm, her voice betrayed her irritation.

'The victim was a dear friend of yours, wasn't she?' he questioned.

'Yes'

'Are you angry at the defendants? Do you hate them?'

'Of course, they…'

Cutting her off, he continued 'Is that why you are giving false testimony in court?

'I am *not* giving false testimony,' she replied.

'Are you aware that if you are proven to have given false testimony in court, you can go to prison? It is contempt of court, as per Section…'

'I am not lying,' she said cutting him off. 'And you can't frighten me. I am a law student. I know all the clauses.'

He gave a small smile as he replied, 'I am not trying to frighten you. I am just making sure that you know the consequences of your acts.'

'I am *not* lying!' she repeated.

'When they raped your friend, were they facing you?' he asked.

'No, they were sideways from me,' she replied.

'So you didn't see their faces properly, did you?'

'After he (here she looked at Raghav) was finished I realized that the rest of them intended to rape her as well. So I ran a few steps in their direction. That's when he stood up and started walking towards me and I saw his face properly. I thought that he had seen me as well. I got scared and ran back inside the lane. But he had not seen me because I was in the dark. I had already seen the faces of the rest when he was raping Sandhya. They were looking around, trying to ensure that nobody saw them.'

'How convenient,' he replied with a small laugh. 'You saw them but they didn't see you. How is that even possible?'

'I have told you, I was hiding behind the tree,' she replied, evidently exasperated.

'But later you say you ran towards them, right? What time did this incident take place?' he questioned.

'About eleven p.m.,' she replied.

'And you have already said that it was dark?'

'Yes, but there were street lights,' she replied.

'Did the rape happen below the street light?' he inquired pointedly.

'No. But there was enough light for me to see what was happening clearly,' she replied.

'There was enough light for you to see them, but not enough for them to see you when you ran towards them?' he questioned.

'I saw everything clearly,' she repeated.

'You saw everything clearly,' he repeated questioningly.

'Yes,' she replied with confidence.

Here he paused for dramatic effect, as though he was contemplating something of great importance. Then he started asking questions again.

'Can you describe the colour of your friend's underwear?' he asked.

'What?' Janaki asked. She was obviously disturbed by this question. She had not expected that anything like that would be asked. She looked at the public prosecutor, shocked, but he did not object. Then she looked at the judge, but he did not seem to find anything objectionable either. He was looking at her sternly, expecting her to respond.

'Answer my question. You said you saw everything clearly. Did you see it?' the defence lawyer prodded.

Janaki sat there staring at him, still unable to reply.

'Did you…' he repeated.

'No' she replied, still looking shocked.

'Why not?' he inquired.

'Because they were raping her,' she replied in a muffled voice.

'That's why you should have been able to see it, right?' he asked in a quiet voice.

'But…but I don't remember,' she said betraying her confusion. 'I mean, it was too far for me to see that…it was…'

'So your memory is affected. You don't remember everything clearly as you claimed, do you?' he questioned.

'I didn't see this,' she replied.

'Yes, you didn't see it as it was too far, wasn't it? It was on the other side of the wide main road. You couldn't see properly.'

'I saw them properly. I only couldn't see her properly,' she replied in a low voice.

'How convenient,' he replied.

'It's true,' she hit back but the earlier conviction was not there in her voice.

Here he took another pause.

Then he asked, 'What clothes were you wearing?

'What relevance does that even have to the murder?' she shouted at him.

He continued without looking at her, 'You were in a suburb of Pune at eleven in the night. The forensic reports state that your friend was wearing jeans. No decent woman would do that. Your friend approached my clients and seduced them and induced them to have illicit intercourse with her. Later, she asked for money, which they refused to pay. So she tried to blackmail them. When they did not fall prey to her threats, she went away and committed suicide. You threw away the knife and now you are trying to implicate them, aren't you? How disgusting and cheap can you get?'

'That is stupid, preposterous, not true, not true at all,' she shouted, tears in her eyes.

'How much money did you think you would make by trapping my clients? How much did your friend lose?' he asked in a stern voice.

'There is no truth in that. She was raped,' Janaki shouted again but I knew that it was in vain.

He ignored her and went on to address the judge. 'Your Honour, such women are a curse to society. They destroy families and marriages. They have no sense of morality and dignity. My clients are good men who work hard to earn their living. The deceased was an immoral woman and such women go against our cultural values. In our culture, a woman is a mother, a goddess. She is a symbol of purity...'

He continued in this vein. Janaki sat there, shocked. And I was as shocked as her. I couldn't help staring at the defence lawyer, listening as he defamed the little girl whom I had known all her life. And I wondered if the world had gone crazy.

The defence counsel condemned Sandhya using the most eloquent language. She was being called 'cheap' only because she had been outside her house at eleven at night. Only because she had been wearing jeans. Only because she had demanded the right to live her life. I looked at her parents sitting next to me and I cannot describe their expression; parents who, having lost their daughter to the violence and depravity of others, were having to listen to utterances intended to entirely sully the dignity of their daughter.

The defence lawyer had a very exhaustive vocabulary of objectionable words which he generously utilized, stopping just short of actually calling Sandhya a prostitute, but making it clear that was what he thought. I couldn't help thinking that our culture is hailed for making women goddesses, but the truth is that it forgets that women are humans, and thus deprives them of their basic human rights. And that the defence counsel, while giving lectures about morality, considered it appropriate to use any means, however immoral, to score his point. No one stood up and pointed this out. The public prosecutor did not object. The honourable judge...he found it amusing and kept shooting glances at Janaki.

This is maybe why I find this profession despicable. But Janaki who was sitting there, shocked, entered the same profession.

There was pin-drop silence in the car as we drove back home. Janaki was sitting next to me in the back. Her eyes were red and it looked as if she was still holding back more tears. I held her hand and she did not shake it off, but she refused to meet my eyes.

When we reached home, she went into her room and shut the door. Anita, Partha and I each tried to speak to her, but she didn't respond. She was lying on her bed, and drew away from me when I tried to comfort her. I was saddened by this but thought that I should respect her wishes. She had faced enough trauma already. I had to give her some space if that was what she wanted.

I went to Shridhar's room. He had refused to come to the court. When he saw me, he realized that something had gone wrong. He asked me about the morning in a concerned tone and I told him about the ordeal Janaki had had to endure in court

'Did she talk to you afterwards?' he asked, knowing

Janaki's habit of keeping silent about things that hurt her. I shook my head and he sighed.

When I returned to the living room, I saw Rahul going in to speak to Janaki. I expected that he, too, would come out soon. But he sat inside with her for a long time. I could hear his voice, speaking softly, and after some time, I could hear Janaki's voice respond. Feeling lighter now that she was speaking to someone, I quietly went to my house.

15

THE TRIAL DRAGGED ON. AFTER DELIVERING HIS SPEECH, the defence counsel was unable to attend court a number of times and thus new dates had to be granted. The public prosecutor, already overburdened, also missed a couple of dates. Partha and Anita could not attend all the hearings due to the demands of their jobs. I, being retired, had all the time in the world and I wanted to give Janaki all the moral support I could, especially after what had happened when she gave her testimony. Thus, Janaki, I and Sandhya's parents began to attend the hearings together. I was a stranger to them, but as time passed we got to know each other very well and I always assured them that the murderers of their daughter would receive severe punishment. Rahul used to come with us whenever he could spare the time.

Three years passed, but not much progress was made on the case. 'Be patient' was the only answer we received to any question. Initially, Janaki had made it a point to go to court every time there was a hearing. But later, she, too, stopped. 'It's of no use,' she told me. So in the end, it was only Sandhya's parents who faithfully came to every hearing.

By 2010, Janaki had completed her education. She started working as a junior lawyer in Pune. Rahul had managed to get admission in an engineering college, also in Pune. The events of that night had affected him as well, and he ended up giving only one of the three entrance examinations that he had planned to. He was by that time in the fourth and final year of college. Life goes on, you see. It went on for everyone except Sandhya's parents. They were obviously frustrated.

In the meantime, Mohan had been released from the observation home. The Juvenile Justice Board had not reached a conclusion about his participation in the rape, but the maximum punishment under the Juvenile Justice Act is three years. He had stayed in the observation home for more than three years, so his lawyers appealed and he was released. He started attending the hearings, a fact which Sandhya's parents found extremely distressing. One of the persons who had raped and killed their daughter was not only free, but he demonstrated no feeling of remorse, and was sitting in court offering support to his adult companions in the brutality. They, however, were not released. Had they been rich, getting bail might not have been a problem. Being poor and thus unable to pay the amount required as security for the capital offense of murder, they remained in jail. However, this provided Sandhya's parents some relief.

I had started going to meet Shridhar at his house every evening. Our morning walks together had stopped as he no longer left the house. He seemed to have aged rapidly ever since that fateful night. He had lost all his hair and always seemed to be exhausted, sapped of all strength. He preferred to stay at home and I had to go for my walks alone.

At first, he had been very eager to know about any progress in the case, as he had known Sandhya since her childhood and was disturbed and scared by what had happened to her. But over time, his interest began to reduce and he seemed to have given up. When I asked him to accompany me to the court once, he refused. He found the whole matter very distressing and would literally shut his eyes every time it was mentioned. I used give him company from about six o'clock in the evening, till Janaki came home, at about eight-thirty. Then, I used to sit with her for some time before leaving.

I say 'sit with her' because we didn't talk much. If I had gone to court that day, she used to inquire what had happened, though telling her about it did not usually take much time. Otherwise, we used to discuss the weather—not even the news, just the weather. Our lengthy conversations seemed to have become a thing of the distant past. Janaki, too, had stopped talking.

In June 2010, she was summoned again to court. The public prosecutor told Janaki that he wanted to clear up some points which he had missed during the direct examination. I went with her. Sandhya's parents were also, of course, there, and so was Mohan. But the defence counsel was unable to appear and sent a note with his junior stating he was unwell and requesting a future date. The request was obviously granted and Janaki did not give testimony.

Janaki went out of the courtroom without saying a word. I waited and tried to speak with the public prosecutor. Before I could say anything, he just looked at me and said that such delays were routine and that I should be patient. There was clearly no point in talking to him, so I left. I looked for Janaki as I emerged from the building. She was waiting for me near the gate and saw me. As she came towards me, she was intercepted by Mohan, who whispered something in her ear. She stared at him when he had stopped whispering. Then he whispered a few more words and was gone. She stood for a moment staring at his back, and then she shook her head and came up to me.

'What was Mohan saying?' I asked her, concerned.

'Nothing special, Ajoba,' she replied, and then when I continued looking at her questioningly, she added, 'I think he expects me to not give testimony against his friends.'

'But you have already given your testimony,' I replied, puzzled.

'Well, he expects that I should retract my earlier statement,' she replied with a sigh.

'Is he threatening you?' I asked, alarmed.

'No, not really,' she answered in an emotionless voice. 'All he said is that coming home from a suburb at eight-thirty at night, as he knows I do every day, can be very dangerous. And he advised me to take precautions for my safety.'

'Janaki, he is threatening you! Can't you see he is threatening you?' I cried out loud. 'Let's go to the police. Let's ask for police protection. This is a threat!'

'A veiled threat, Ajoba,' she replied. 'A veiled threat. He just told me to take care, and he has every right to do so. I don't see either the police or the courts being interested in giving me protection. And if I approach the court, he will claim that he was just making a statement for my benefit and safety. He did not ask me to change my testimony and there is no evidence that he is threatening me. It's just my word against his. And he did not say that he will kill me if I didn't change my testimony. No, Ajoba, I will not get protection for this. It will only make me more vulnerable.'

'But then what can we do?' I asked her, feeling helpless.

For a minute she didn't respond. Then she looked at me and said, 'I couldn't save Sandhya, Ajoba. But I will try to make sure that she gets justice. No matter who says what to me.'

She crossed the road to find a rickshaw for us to go home. It was just about one o'clock at that time.

In the evening, I went to meet Shridhar. Janaki was not there but Partha and Anita were. Rahul came home just a few moments after I reached the house. He looked around for his sister. I remembered when I saw him that it was Rahul who had managed to soothe his sister after the shock that she had endured while giving her testimony. He had given her the mental support she needed then. That day, he was naturally anxious to know what had happened in court. He must have been hoping that his sister had not been forced to suffer another attack from the same eloquent speaker once again. He looked at me questioningly and I told him that she had gone to work.

I could see that the entire family was naturally curious about what had happened in court. Janaki had not called any of them, and they, too, had not called her, afraid that it might disturb her. They knew that if anything too bad had happened, then I would have immediately let them know. They assumed that everything was all right, especially after I told them that the defence lawyer had not turned up.

At first, I hesitated to tell them about Mohan's warning

to Janaki. I didn't want to scare them, especially not Shridhar whose health had deteriorated so much. I was scared that he would panic. But after mulling it over, I decided that they needed to know. It was too serious a thing for me to keep it from them. Maybe I also hoped that they would somehow stop her, change her mind, where I couldn't. I was very scared for her. So I told them.

It did indeed scare them all, and they waited restlessly for Janaki to come back home. Anita wanted to call Janaki, but was finally persuaded not to, because Partha pointed out that if they asked her about it over the phone, she would get annoyed and would come home later than usual. They decided to wait until she returned to speak to her.

We all waited for her in the living room. Shridhar sat in his usual armchair with his eyes closed and his hand stroking his beard, with me to his left. Rahul was on the sofa to my left, apparently engrossed in thought and not looking at anyone. Partha and Anita were opposite me, with their backs to the wall. Every five minutes they would turn and look anxiously at the clock on the wall.

When Janaki finally came home, she looked at the frightened expressions on her parents' faces and then at me. She knew that I had told them what had happened. She went straight into her room without saying a word.

After a few minutes, she came out and sat down on the sofa next to her brother. Nobody spoke. Partha cleared his throat a number of times but didn't say anything. Rahul was looking at his sister intently.

In the end, it was Janaki who spoke. Her voice sounded

cold as she said, 'No matter who threatens me and no matter what warnings I get, I am going to give testimony in court and I am not going to change what I have already stated. I am also not going to sit at home due to fear. My decision is final and I expect you to support it.' Saying this, she looked at her parents, then at her grandfather who had again closed his eyes. She had stood up to return to her room when she was stopped by her father.

'Janaki, stop. Listen to us.' he said, his voice pleading. She turned and looked directly at him. After taking a deep breath, he continued, 'We know that Sandhya was very close to you. I...we are very sorry that she died. But we have to look ahead. We don't want you to get hurt. We are...'

'I won't get hurt' she interrupted in an emotionless voice. 'I will be fine. Nothing is going to happen to me. I am...'

'What are you saying, Janaki?' Shridhar shouted angrily. We all jumped and turned to stare at him. Lately, he had almost stopped talking, much less thundering like this. His eyes were no longer closed and he was leaning forward and staring intensely at her. 'What are you saying?' he repeated. 'He has threatened you. He has already killed once and he will do it again. These people are murderers, Janaki, they...'

'Exactly,' she replied calmly. 'They are murderers and they deserve to go to jail.'

'Janaki,' Partha said exasperatedly, 'Please stop being so idealistic. We want Sandhya's murderers to go to jail too. But we have to be practical here, okay? Please at least listen to us without getting angry. We love you and we care about you. That is why we are saying this. I know you are hurt.

But can't you see? If you testify, they'll kill you as well. We must think rationally now. Keep your emotions aside. It is not worth taking a risk.'

'Sandhya was murdered,' said Janaki, her voice rising with every word. Tears accumulated in her eyes as she repeated, '*Murdered*, Baba. And you tell me it's not worth the risk? Her murderers will walk free. Do you understand that? And it is *not* about emotions. It's about justice. You are telling me to forget that and be practical?'

'Janaki, it's too dangerous!' Partha cried out.

'Well, now you are also sounding like those waiters and the manager who did not help me. "Let's be practical," they said. "Taking panga with goons is not good for business. Let the girl die." You want me to be like them? No, I won't be like them. Even if I die, I will…'

'Enough, Janaki, I have heard enough,' Shridhar interrupted loudly, getting up from his chair. He looked even more agitated than Janaki. He continued speaking, harshly and unevenly. 'Stop judging us like this. Stop shouting at us with righteous indignation. Yes, we are like those waiters. We don't want our daughter to die. We are selfish because we do not want you to die.' He took a breath and sat down again. His face had become red. He removed his spectacles and wiped his eyes on the sleeve of his kurta and continued in a shaky voice, 'I have lived a long and hard life. We didn't have any comforts when we were young, nothing. I struggled. Do you have any idea how I managed to complete my education? I used to live in a small, cramped room with my uncle and his family of seven. I struggled and I fought hard. The country had just got independence and it was not easy. I became a doctor and worked night and day at all odd hours to build a home. I got married. Your grandmother saved as much money as possible. We struggled, we sacrificed, so that our children would get a better life. So that you would have all comforts. So that you won't have to struggle the way we did. I did not struggle my entire life to see my granddaughter commit suicide. It's me who has the right to die. You don't have that right. You have to live because I sacrificed so many things to see you live. I will not let you commit suicide, I will not, I will not.'

He stopped talking but continued shaking his head. I don't remember ever seeing him as distressed as he was that day. He had started looking so much older in those three years. His eyes had become red and his lips were trembling. I was shocked to see him like that. He kept on murmuring 'I will not let you die,' under his breath.

Nobody spoke. We had not expected Shridhar to say what he did. Partha and Anita exchanged glances. I touched Shridhar's shoulder, but he did not notice. Janaki was staring at the ceiling. Rahul was nervously fidgeting and looking first at Janaki, then at Shridhar. Five minutes passed, then ten. Janaki came and sat down on the sofa again. There was pin-drop silence.

Then Janaki spoke. There were no tears in her eyes anymore. Her voice was firm and resolute. She said to Shridhar, 'I love you Aba, and I don't want to hurt you. You don't want me to die and I don't want to die either. But what about Sandhya? Her grandparents are your age. They also struggled, just like you. And they didn't struggle to see their granddaughter die. But she is dead. The idea that I can die hurts you. How will they feel when they are denied justice because of me? They will be shattered. They...'

'I don't care how they will feel, okay?' Shridhar shouted back, looking tired and angry at the same time. 'I only know that you are killing yourself and I am going to stop you from doing that. I don't care about anything else. You are not going to die. I don't care about how anybody else feels. I don't care. I don't...'

'That's the problem. You don't care about anything else,' she said, pointing at Shridhar. 'You don't care' she said, her voice loud and harsh. 'As long as your granddaughter is not killed, you don't care. Let somebody else die. You will just feel sorry for a few minutes and then forget. You will feel lucky that it is not you and you will forget. Of course you don't care!'

'Janaki, we know you are distressed,' Partha tried to mollify her. 'We are sorry that Sandhya died...'

'Oh! Yes, you are sorry,' she cut him off. 'But you don't care! You won't do anything until the situation hurts you personally. You say you were against the British rule, Aba. But why? Because it hurt you, made you poor. But casteism? Farmers committing suicide? Women being raped? Doesn't hurt you, so you don't care. Yes, you know all the numbers, all the statistics. Your favourite pastime. But as long as it doesn't touch you, you are fine. You don't care.'

She paused and bit her lower lip. Her eyes were filled with tears again. She gulped and the continued in the same harsh voice, 'Sandhya died? "Oh! We are so sorry," you say. But you will not "let" your daughter, your granddaughter, try to get justice for her, will you? No. It shocks you when it touches you, shakes you up. I was also there with Sandhya at the same place, at the same time. I could have been the one murdered and she could have been the witness. And then, if she had given false testimony, how would you have felt then? Think about it.'

Shridhar had crossed his arms and was not looking at her. Partha opened his mouth and closed it again without saying anything. Janaki gave a sigh and continued, 'Can't I even do this for her? Can't I even give testimony? I did not save her. I did not risk my life. I just hid myself. I saw her being raped and I hid myself. And that's going to eat me from inside for the rest of my life. Don't I even have the courage to give my testimony? She tried to fight; she went down fighting for her life. There were three of them then, but she fought. And I? There is only one person now. He said something vague to me and am I such a coward to get scared by that? I can't fight with even one person? And for all you know, he may just have been bluffing. Yes, it is just a bluff. It's not that easy to kill. '

She took another deep breath and said, 'And you say that you don't care. It's okay for you if your granddaughter is a coward, but she should not come under any threat. You know what? It may be okay for you, but it is not okay for me. Can't I even stand up to a little pressure? I am done with being a coward. This time, I am going to stand up. I don't care what kind of threats I get. And I am sorry that you don't care.'

She stopped speaking and there was absolute silence.

Her cheeks had become pink and her lips had drained of all colour. She was hugging herself. Her eyes were clear and no longer red but filled with determination. She looked around as though challenging any one to speak against her, and no one did. Partha and Anita were shocked. They had not expected the onslaught. Their daughter had always been a mild and soft-spoken girl. Partha was shaking his head. Anita was looking at her lap. Shridhar was leaning back in his armchair and had closed his eyes. Rahul, however, was staring at his sister unblinkingly, intent.

When Janaki addressed us again, she looked almost serene. She looked at her grandfather once and then addressing her parents, she said, 'I love you, all of you. I don't want to hurt any of you. But my decision is final. If you don't want to support me, it's okay. But don't try to stop me because my mind is made up.' She returned to her room.

Shridhar had not opened his eyes. I patted him on the shoulder but he did not respond. Partha got up and went into his bedroom, while Anita entered the kitchen. Rahul sat there for a while, looking at Shridhar nervously. Then he followed his sister inside the room. The siblings had one of their long conversations and when their mother called them out for dinner after some time, they seemed to be on very good terms. Janaki later told me that Rahul had supported her decision not to bow to the threats.

True to her word, Janaki did not change her testimony. But the threats affected her. Mohan had acquired her cell phone number and he started giving missed calls from different PCOs late at night. He never directly threatened her. He didn't even call every night. But he was keeping an eye on all her activities and he knew exactly where she was, what she did the entire day, who she was with and when she came home. And he let her know that he was trailing her. When she started turning off her phone at night while sleeping, he started stalking her. He knew where she worked and he started waiting at the bus stop just opposite her office. Janaki used to usually travel by bus as it was too far to go there by two-wheeler or rickshaw. At first, he just used to come and stand next to her when she waited there for the bus. But once he got on the bus with her and followed her home. She finally had to apply for a restraining order from the court to prevent him from stalking her.

Though she ignored all this, it took a toll on her health. She had black circles under her eyes and was under constant stress. She could not concentrate. She made serious mistakes in her work, and was fired. She did not speak about how she felt about this to anyone. I tried to talk to her about it but she wouldn't respond. She only requested her parents to support her as she took some months off. They agreed. They'd tried to talk to her, to help her, but she didn't respond. The only person who could get through to her was Rahul. They had many chats together, but he refused to say anything to us about them either.

She kept her word. On the next day of the hearing, she gave all the details to the public prosecutor and withstood the cross-examination of the defence counsel, who stated again that she and Sandhya were 'cheap women'. However, the judge had changed by that time. He had been replaced by a female judge who told the defence counsel, basically to shut up and not pursue his strategy of defaming the deceased. He was thus forced to ask a few abrupt questions and Janaki was allowed to leave.

Janaki did not become a 'coward'. She stood up. She kept her promise. Unfortunately for her, Mohan was not bluffing either. He kept his word too…

In our society, men believe that they have the moral right to give orders and it is inconceivable for them that a woman might dare to say no. Mohan never thought that he and his friends were wrong to have attacked Sandhya. Janaki's resistance to him resulted in a furious desire for revenge as, in his view, she had wronged him, and so, she was the culprit.

He tried to hurt her, take revenge. But it was difficult. She had changed her phone number and had stopped going to office. She used to sit at home all day, going out only in the evening, for a walk in the nearby hills, and that too with her brother or father. She was never alone and so Mohan did not get a chance to take revenge. Thus, he did what criminals usually do. He did not hurt her directly. He chose an unsuspecting victim, a soft target. He hit a person not involved in anything, someone who had committed no wrong, just to hurt her.

JANAKI

16

I GAVE MY TESTIMONY FOR THE SECOND TIME IN JULY. That year, 2010, I had turned twenty-six. August, my birth month, used to be my favourite month. It is also the time for Ganeshotsav, an important festival in Pune.

There are many public and community Ganpatis in Pune. This tradition, celebrating the festival not only in one's homes but also on a community level, was started by the late freedom fighter and leader Lokmanya Tilak, with the aim of uniting people against the British rule. The British are gone, but the tradition continues. There has been a drastic increase in the number of Ganpati mandals over the years. But the five most important Ganpatis, the traditional and oldest ones, known as 'Manache Ganpati' or 'respected Ganpatis', are still the most prestigious. Every year, thousands of people come to Pune to witness the festival. The crowds are the biggest on the tenth, and last, day of the festival, known as Anantchaturdashi. On this day, the idols are carried in procession to be immersed in the river. There is music, gulal and celebration, accompanied by a prayer to the Lord to come sooner next year.

The river, Mutha, runs through the centre of Pune and divides it into two. At one time it used to provide water to the city directly, but now it is dammed in several places. The dams then provide water. When the remaining water reaches the city, it is still used—but rather differently, as a convenient outlet for sewage and garbage. The two parts of the city are joined by many bridges. The main procession of the idols goes over one of the oldest bridges, known as Sambhaji Bridge or Lakdi Pul. The bridge was originally made of wood supposedly by the Peshwas in the eighteenth century. After crossing this bridge, the procession continues parallel to the river till the idols finally reach the place for immersion. Most of the largest idols are actually not immersed in the river, as that would pollute the already over-polluted water to such an extent that it would be impossible to live in the city. Once the procession reaches full swing in the evening, the roads are completely jam-packed with traffic and onlookers.

So it was August. The month of my birth. The month of Ganeshotsav. By all auspices, a fortunate month. But I am not fortunate. Unlike Camus's Outsider, who is not sure about the day his mother died, I unfortunately know all too well when and how my mother died. I was with her in her last moments. The doctors said that she died of pneumonia. Rahul and I, we don't agree.

On Anantchaturdashi, all schools and colleges are shut. That year, my mother, too, had given a day off to her students. Private offices often remain open, but many of them give half the day off to their employees, to let them reach home before the procession starts in the afternoon. My father was expected home for lunch. My brother was in his fourth year of college, so he had a holiday. For me, unemployed and home-bound, that day was like any other.

My mother had gone out. Her sister had just returned after six months in the US with her daughter, who had just had her first child. Rahul and I were expected to go with my mother to visit her, but I had refused. Every meeting with family members would inevitably lead to the topic of marriage. Or, more aptly, to the topic of my lack of interest in getting married. My family used to go on and on about the importance of marriage and how time was running out for me, which I found unbearably irritating. So I refused to accompany my mother and Rahul stayed at home to give me company.

My mother was expected home by lunch, as she did not want to get stuck in the traffic. But Madhuri Maushi and she had a lot to talk about, so Maushi insisted that she should eat there, especially as the special foods that are traditionally served on this day of the festival had been made in their house. My mother rang us up to say she would come home immediately afterwards, but she was delayed yet again. A relative of ours who stays near my aunt's house came to visit them. By the time my mother actually left my aunt's house, it was six in the evening and the procession had reached full swing.

It so happens that my aunt lives in the centre of the city where the procession begins, while our house is on the opposite bank of the river. The closest and fastest route between the two houses goes via Lakdi Pul, which was crowded with the idols and their accompanying devotees that day. However, because of the procession, traffic had been diverted to the other bridges so they, too, were jammed. My mother thought it best to come home on foot instead of hiring a rickshaw as she had originally planned to do. As it must have been quite impossible to walk through the throng on Lakdi Pul, she decided to go home via a causeway. She never reached home.

Ganeshotsav served to unite people against the British Raj. Today, it still proposes unity, but it is also a soft target for terrorist attacks. That is why extra police personnel from the reserve force are pressed into service around the city at this time every year. It was these policemen who found my mother and rescued her from the river, which was flowing with its full monsoon force. It was they who called us, saying that she had been taken to the hospital. Water had entered her lungs and she had pneumonia. We were all there with her till her last breath.

Three days later, in the early hours of morning, the doctor told us that my mother had died. But it wasn't pneumonia that took her.

The post-mortem report was prepared, with the cause of death being pneumonia. But it also mentioned that there were bruises on her wrists, upper arms and mouth. The marks on her cheeks showed that she might have been gagged. There is a possibility that she may have been thrown into the water. There are no proper railings, so it wouldn't have been too difficult to push her in. Even if she had managed to shout, no one would have heard her, due to the noise of the procession. No one would have seen her either, as the causeway was at a much lower height than the main bridge and, in any case, everyone would have been engrossed in the procession.

The river was very high and fast at that season. My mother was found downstream, a considerable distance from the causeway. The current was strong enough to have washed away any fingerprints on her body or cloth on her face. The bruises could have been made earlier, by accident, or during her time at the mercy of the current. The whole thing could have been an accident. Or, as the police officer was kind enough to remind us in a dispassionate voice, it could have been a suicide. In any case, it was clear that there was no evidence for the police to open an investigation.

My father and brother wanted to save me the pain of having to attend a second cremation within four years. They'd forgotten that the person being cremated was my mother. They were scared that I would break down. But I didn't. We teach our boys to be strong. We need to teach our girls to be strong and our boys how to express emotions. But the reason I did not break down was not that I was strong. It was because I was numb, in a trance. My relatives cried and I stared at them. When I didn't cry, they felt that I didn't care about my mother. They felt that I had become an outsider. But unfortunately, I am not that, either.

Afterwards, I returned home and went to my grandfather. His health had deteriorated further and he hadn't attended the cremation. After holding hands with him for a few minutes, I went to the room I shared with my brother. He was not there. I sat on my bed and stared at the wall opposite. I didn't know what to do. I just sat staring at the wall, which my mother had convinced my father to paint blue, to please me. I was sitting there when my brother came in, crying. He put his head on my lap and I patted it. I continued to stare at the wall. After some time, he got up. He might have said something to me, I don't remember. Then he went out, leaving me still staring at the wall.

Then Ajoba came in. My grandfather's closest friend. A man whom I trusted implicitly. But I didn't notice him. It was only when he had put his arm around my shoulder that I noticed his presence. I rested my head on his shoulder and somehow, it made me come out my trance. I did not cry—I wailed. I cried with my stomach, my lungs. I could feel the sobs coming from my navel, moving upwards till they reached my throat and turned into a wail.

When I was a kid I used to get seizures. The doctors classified it as epilepsy, but the symptoms were rather different from classical epilepsy. They were not as violent, nor was there that split second of clarity before the fit which epileptic patients describe. But it was a seizure nevertheless. I still remember how it felt. Before the seizure, I would stop breathing. Even if I tried to breathe, I couldn't. It felt as though my lungs had no space to expand, as though they had been put in a kind of a cage. My air pipe seemed to contract, leaving no space for air to come in. My nose seemed to get blocked. I was given medicines and these seizures stopped. But that day, when I started crying, I experienced these symptoms again. I did not faint or have a fit, but I experienced the same inability to breathe, and a hollowness in my heart, like a well. And from this well my periodic sobs were drawn out. They were not like a volcano bursting; it took effort even to cry. Often, after crying, one feels better. I didn't. I felt as though I was going deeper and deeper into my misery, down into one layer after another. I felt as though I would collapse from within.

All my childhood memories of my mother, the way she spoke to us and looked at us, overwhelmed me. I tried to block out the memories, but I couldn't. All our happy memories, they just came and I couldn't stop them. Later, I welcomed them. Memories were all that I had. Even her ashes were gone. Pain is better than numbness, I know. But how I wish I could be numb again.

That evening, my brother and I sneaked out of the house and went for a walk on our beloved hill. Pune has small hills right in the centre of the city, offering a nice place to walk. Some, like Parvati or Vetal tekdi, are thickly forested. During the rains they display an incredible range of colours, including an enviable variety of green. There are peacocks and rabbits and a fascinating variety of smaller birds in these forests. But we did not go to those hills.

We went to a hill with two names: Hanuman tekdi and Fergusson College hill. It is called Hanuman tekdi because there is a Hanuman temple on the top. It is also called Fergusson College hill because one of the oldest colleges of this city, the Fergusson College, is located at its foot. At one time, it was connected to Vetal tekdi, but now this connection is broken by an extremely busy road. Vetal tekdi has always had forest cover in my lifetime, so much so that one may feel that one is somewhere far away, at least for some time. And then, of course, one hears loud honking noises from the adjacent road and the city rushes back. Hanuman tekdi is the opposite of this. Despite being completely deforested, the efforts of some nature lovers and the municipal corporation (which hesitatingly and belatedly gave help) led to some trees being planted on the hill. Today, the forest cover has increased but still is much less than on the other hills.

The reason why we went here, the reason why I like this hill more than the others, is because one will always be able to see the city from the top. Our concrete jungle near the real jungle. I love this city with its lights, its energy, and despite its violence. I am a city girl. I was born in this city, so were my parents and my grandparents. My roots are in this city. My native place? This city.

The city engulfs you. It provides a warm cloak of anonymity. You can disappear in the crowd. You can cry your heart out without anybody disturbing you—even looking at you. You can laugh like a madman. Nobody tries to save you. Nobody bothers you.

I am a lawyer. We have to draft legal documents, like deeds and contracts, based on the model drafts prepared by senior lawyers. All you have to do is to change the particulars in the model draft. In the city, there is a model draft for every relationship, a format we must follow. This draft is in our head. The conversations are premeditated. We are taught what to say, to whom and in what circumstance. And it is so ingrained within us that it becomes instinctive. We think that these are our own inner responses. If we don't respond appropriately, others are alarmed. If I don't cry softly at my mother's cremation—or if I wail later—people are alarmed.

In the city, our relationships are of interdependence and convenience. When our loved ones die, our friends and acquaintances offer condolences and we accept them, knowing that there is no feeling involved behind them. We act in the same way when it's our turn. My friend's mother died? Okay. But why should I feel sad? I don't. But then why should I say I'm sorry? Because I have been taught to. And because I feel guilty.

Are all feelings lost? Are all relationships simply those of convenience? No. My relationship with my mother was not one of convenience. I loved her. When she died, it hurt. But did it hurt because I really loved her, or because I have been taught that it ought to hurt me? Am I simply following the model draft of responses in my head? Is my hurt out of guilt or is it out of habit? I don't know. I don't know the difference between what I feel and what I have been taught to feel; I cannot differentiate because I never knew. To know this, I have to be able to see my face in the mirror. I can't. I never have. I have always only seen a mask.

The city provides you with a wide range of masks to wear. We change the masks according to our training and without even noticing. I will never be able to live in a village. Not because I have never lived in one. Not because I don't know how to farm. But because I would not know which mask to wear. There will be a completely different set of masks there.

And there is one more difference: maybe, unlike in cities, if I live in a village, in certain conditions, I will not have to wear any masks at all. I will see my face in the mirror without a mask. What a scary proposition!

No, I don't want to go to the village. My concrete jungle is fine. It allows me to be alone; it allows me to be lonely. For we are lonely, always, inevitably. The city only prevents me from believing in the illusion of not being lonely. It destroys the myth that we can run away from loneliness. We are born alone, to live our lives alone. We experience birth alone. We experience death alone. In the middle, we try to build relationships to create an illusion of not being alone. Cities are blamed for making us individualistic, for making us lonely. It is not true. We are individualistic, we are lonely. The city just exposes the truth. It destroys these relationships and releases us from our illusions. It forces us to see that we are going to die alone.

Life can be interpreted only through death. It can be given meaning only by death. If death is lonely, then so is life. The city prevents me from running away from this fact. And that is why I love this city.

If my mother had died at the age of ninety, we would have said that she had a full life. And when I grow old and die, others will say the same. But I don't suffer from illusions. I am comfortable, within myself. I get my space. I wear my masks and use the model draft of responses all the time without caring. I can just vanish and everything will go on as though nothing has changed.

AJOBA

17

I COMFORTED JANAKI THAT DAY AFTER HER MOTHER'S cremation. In the evening, she and Rahul disappeared somewhere. I was with Shridhar. He was in shock. I sat with him, speaking words of comfort, but I knew that they made no sense to him. And they made no sense to me either. I said them because I did not know what else to do. Because they were supposed to be said.

Janaki started searching for jobs the very next day. It seemed to me as though she just wanted to get out of the house. By the next month, she had started a new job and I had begun to stay the whole day with Shridhar, whose health had become even worse after Anita's death. When Janaki started going to office, I used to miss her.

Rahul used to be at home sometimes. He had started bunking classes ever since his mother's death. After that, he had become sullen and withdrawn and hardly talked to anyone. He locked himself in his room and almost never came out. Partha tried to reach out to him, but failed. He had never been a hands-on father. Anita had always been his medium of communication with the children. And he was also traumatized. His will power could take him no further.

The only person in the family with whom Rahul spoke openly was his sister. They continued to have conversations. He also had a close friend who talked with him and managed to convince him to start attending college again. Apart from going to his classes, he would only go out with his sister, to the hill nearby. This was their tradition for a few months, and then it was broken.

We had all already realized that court cases can be traumatic after seeing Janaki's experience on the witness stand. But unfortunately, she had to give testimony in court once more, and in a different case. She was again the primary witness for the prosecution. But this time, the defendant was her beloved brother.

JANAKI

18

RAHUL AND I CONTINUED TO CLIMB THE HILL OFTEN. October brought a slight chill to the air, but one Sunday evening we decided to go up to the hill. On our way back down, we saw Mohan. The trial was still going on, so his cousin and Mohammed Ali remained in jail, but he was free to wander around Pune. When I saw him from a distance, I first felt scared, but almost immediately, I told myself that I had already given the testimony so he could do nothing to intimidate me anymore. Or so I thought. I was glad that my brother was with me, and that there were many other people climbing up and coming down on the path. At least that meant he wouldn't dare to do anything, I thought. He did not threaten me, did not say a word till I passed, just stared at me. But when I was almost out of earshot, he said loudly, 'How is your mother? Is she alright? The water can be quite cold in this season. I hope she can swim.'

Before I knew it, Rahul had turned and hit him in the face. There was a scuffle between the two of them. I held Rahul back with great difficulty and some of the passers-by also intervened to stop the fight. Rahul started screaming abuses at Mohan till he disappeared into the woods. He shook me off, and started following him. I tried to stop him, saying, 'It's no use, Rahul!' but he kept going. I ran after him, pleading. 'Please, Rahul, please stop.' I begged. 'Please.' He stared at me for a moment and then returned, and we resumed walking back down the hill.

When we reached the place where the fight had taken place, we saw that the people who had intervened were still there. As they saw Rahul coming back, one of them tried to speak to him, but he glared so ferociously that it frightened and silenced the man. As I passed him, I apologized and thanked him for intervening. He nodded and started walking again.

On our way back, Rahul didn't say a word. When we reached home, he went and locked himself inside our room. I told my father what had happened. He decided to go and report the matter to the police. We hoped that Mohan's taunts would be enough for them to start an investigation into my mother's death. But, even then, I knew that such hopes were unrealistic.

Some time after my father left, I was finally able to persuade Rahul to open the door. I sat next to him and held his hand. Then I told him that our father had gone to the police. His shook his head and said, 'They will not do anything. He killed mom, but they will just tell us that nothing can be done. They will not do anything.' He was getting more and more agitated as he repeated it. Suddenly he punched the cushion and threw it at the opposite wall. Then he started crying. I held him tightly and stroked his hair. I tried to say something comforting, but I couldn't stop crying myself.

After more than two hours, our father came back. It was past eight and it was pitch dark outside. Rahul and I were sitting in the living room waiting for him. Ajoba and my grandfather were still in Aba's room. When my father came in, we got up. He looked at us and shook his head. Then he sat down on the sofa and buried his head in his hands. I went and sat down next to him. I hugged him and I could feel him sobbing. It was the first time in my life that I had seen him cry. Even at my mother's cremation, he had managed to hold up for us. But now he was sobbing and I couldn't do anything. The feeling of numbness which I'd felt at my mother's cremation came back to me. My head felt heavy and I was exhausted. I just kept on hugging him.

After some time, he wiped his tears. 'That bastard,' he murmured and shook his head. 'And they say... they say, there is not enough evidence. He killed my... And...' he broke off, shaking his head and fighting a fresh surge of tears. He stared into space for some time. Then he suddenly got up and went to his room.

I looked around, only to realize that Rahul was not there. He had locked himself in our room again. I tried to call him out again, but he did not respond. I went to look for my father, but he had locked himself in his room as well. Ajoba was still in my grandfather's room, but I did not go in there. I knew that I would have to tell them about what happened with Mohan. And I didn't want to tell my grandfather anything. He was not well and I didn't want him to suffer any more.

After some time, Ajoba came out. He told me that my grandfather was resting and came up to me and hugged me. He asked me something, but I didn't respond because I couldn't understand what he was saying. Then I realized that he was asking me about my job. I nodded to signify that it was fine.

'Are you alright?' he asked.

'Ya,' I replied, faking a smile. I did not want to tell him what had happened either. Telling him was not going to stop my pain. And he would also feel bad. I wanted to at least spare him further pain. I hugged him and he stroked my head. Then he left for his house.

After some time, my father came out of his room again. He asked me where Rahul was and I told him. He tried to speak to him but Rahul would not respond. He came and sat next to me. Neither of us spoke or read or turned on the TV; we just stared into space for more than an hour.

Finally, Rahul emerged from the room and told us that he was going out to meet his friend, Siddharth. Although we were all upset, and didn't want him to be out on his own, we did not object because we thought that being with his friend might make him feel better. Siddharth had been Rahul's best friend throughout his childhood, after Akshay. He had come to our mother's cremation and had persuaded Rahul to return to college after her death. They used to visit each other often. I also often felt that talking to someone outside, someone who wasn't themselves going through all the grief and shock and horror that our family was suffering, would be good for Rahul.

When Rahul didn't come back after a couple of hours, we called his mobile number. It was switched off, so we tried calling Siddharth. He told us that Rahul had come to meet him, but had left just a few minutes before our call came. Since Siddharth lived in the neighbourhood, we thought Rahul must be on his way back and would reach home soon. But when there was no sign of him, we started getting worried. We waited for an hour, trying frantically to call his cell phone, but it was switched off. Then my father called Siddharth again to ask him if Rahul had said anything about going somewhere else. But he could only tell us that Rahul said he was going home. Siddharth went out to look for Rahul in the neighbourhood, while I called Rahul's other friends to check if he was with any of them. But they all said that they had not met him that day.

My grandfather came out after some time. He had started skipping dinner because he thought it would provide some relief for his stomach, eating only curd or milk at night. When he saw us, he looked at us enquiringly, but my father silently indicated that I should not tell him what was going on. We had already decided long ago to not trouble him unless absolutely necessary because he was in a very frail physical state. So we pretended to be sitting and chatting about work. He did not look convinced, but he did not question us further, just got himself a glass of milk from the refrigerator and went back to his room.

Once he left, my father and I went back to speculating about where Rahul could have gone. My father suggested that he might have gone to visit one of our innumerable relatives, but we both felt it was unlikely. Ever since my mother's death, our interactions with the extended family had been negligible. They had wanted to console us, but Rahul and I had deliberately avoided their company. We did not want their pity and sympathy, and we could not tolerate their tears and concern. So Rahul going to meet them was highly unlikely. Further, even if he had, they would have called and informed us that he was there.

We deliberately avoided talking about what had happened the last time around when I was out late at night, but I knew that it was on both of our minds. We were both scared for him and anxious for his safety. 'Maybe he got hurt, maybe someone attacked him,' we said, without referring to the person we thought could have attacked him. Three hours had already passed, and in my mind there was the fear that a person who can murder twice can also murder three times.

Finally, my father stood up abruptly, saying, 'I'm going to the police, I'll make them listen to me this time...' Just then, Rahul finally came home. It was a few minutes past midnight.

He looked terrible—his face was grey and haggard and his eyes were red. He looked as if he was in some kind of a trance. I could barely look at his face. He stared at us and didn't answer when we asked him where he had been. He was simply fixed to one spot for several minutes, speechless. Although he looked so awful, he stood upright. As my fears about what might have happened to him subsided a little, I began to observe his peculiar behaviour. He seemed disoriented, dazed almost, ignoring all our questions and exclamations. Then I noticed that there was blood splattered on his shirt. I was afraid that he'd been in a fight and had got injured, maybe even badly hurt. But when I asked him about the blood, he just stared at me blankly. I went up to him to check if he had any wounds, but he was able to fend me off quite easily, moving quickly to lock himself up in our room again before either of us could stop him.

We didn't know what was happening or what he had been through. I saw the rucksack that he had been carrying had been left on the floor just inside the door. I picked it up automatically, only to have our kitchen knife fall out of it, covered with blood, even on the handle. We did not know whose blood it was, but we suspected that it was not Rahul's. We also suspected that it might have something to do with the spat he'd had with Mohan earlier. But we didn't talk about it, trying to convince ourselves that there must be some other explanation.

We tried to get Rahul to speak to us. But this time, nothing my father or I said or did could persuade him to come out. He stayed locked in until the police came to arrest him, a handful of hours later, before it was even morning.

Rahul was incompetent as a criminal. He had gone in search of Mohan after he left Siddharth's house. He had switched off his phone to prevent it being traced, but there had been witnesses who had seen him with Mohan. He had found Mohan not in some desolate place, but at a katta where several people had been sitting, drinking alcohol. He had taken out his knife in full view and dragged Mohan off, all the time loudly threatening to kill him. The people there had tried to stop him, but once they saw the mad rage on Rahul's face and the knife in his hands, they kept their distance. They were in any case too inebriated to stop him, but they clearly remembered seeing him and the knife. Afterwards, he hadn't thrown away the knife—my mother's favourite kitchen knife, which was sharper than the others. He hadn't washed the blood off it either. The police found it immediately, along with the smears of blood on his bag and shirt. And he'd come straight home, where the police were bound to find him.

They questioned all of us. My father said that Rahul had been at home that entire night. I contradicted him. I told the police all the events of the evening, starting with the encounter on the hill.

I avoided looking at my father as I related the entire series of events because I knew that he was trying to catch my eye. He tried to interrupt me a couple of times, but the investigating officer disregarded his attempts to speak. Finally, he grasped my shoulder in an attempt to stop me from talking, but I wriggled out of his hold and continued to tell the whole story. I only stopped when I had finished narrating everything.

Then I looked at my father and saw the shock and anger on his face. He had thought that I would follow his lead and lie but I hadn't. I looked at Rahul after that, but he didn't seem surprised. He was shaking his head and looked both sad and angry as they took him to the police station.

The police also took me with them at the same time, leaving my father and grandfather to make their own way, but we were taken in two different vehicles to avoid contact between us. By the time I reached the police station, Rahul was nowhere to be seen. I gave my statement again, for the record, and I became a witness again.

I did not go home after recording my statement. I went to Ajoba's house. I did not tell him what had happened, but he could see that something was wrong. He also understood that I wanted to rest and needed some space. He realized that I did not want to talk about it, not yet. He allowed me to stand in his balcony silently, and got me a toffee while he made the bed in the guest room for me.

Later that morning, my father was called by the police to the station and told that they had Rahul in custody, as they had evidence to prove that he had gone out that night. Siddharth had told them that Rahul had come to his place. The mobile phone records also showed that Rahul had switched off his phone while at Siddharth's house. And then there was the evidence of the people who had seen Mohan being dragged away by him, as well as my statement. My father retracted his earlier statement. He said that he did not know anything about the whole affair. He was the principal and only alibi for the defence, and he decided not to testify at all. He said that if he was summoned, he would state that he was ignorant about the whereabouts of his son on that evening. He went to meet Rahul in custody. Then, he went out to engage the best lawyer he could afford to defend Rahul.

When I went home from Ajoba's place in the afternoon, my father was waiting for me. He shouted at me for more than an hour. He called me an idiot and many other names, and yelled his lungs out. For the first time in my life, I was afraid that my father would hit me and hurt me badly. But it was almost as if I wanted him to hit me. I was waiting for the blow. The blow never came; at least not physically. But I lost my family that day.

My father blamed me for Rahul's arrest and stopped speaking to me. I tried to convince him that my testimony didn't really change anything, as there was too much evidence already against Rahul. But he wouldn't talk to me. My grandfather, too, was not able to speak to me. He had gone into shock after the police left, and he had learnt what had happened. When I saw him, I wanted to take him to a doctor, but my father did not allow it. He said that I had lost the right to take any action or responsibility for any member of my family. He stopped me from talking to my grandfather and blamed me for his condition as well. He said that I was no longer his daughter. So I packed my bags and left.

There was only one place where I could go—Ajoba's house. He never asked me what had happened. I think he had already got to know about it from my father. For several days, I did not say a word to him or anyone else. I just locked myself up in his guest room. Ajoba didn't force me to come out or try to talk to me. He only insisted that I should eat, which I obeyed. When I came out of the room four days later, and sat on the sofa, he made a cup of tea for me. He didn't ask me any questions and waited for me to talk. After a couple of sips, I finally found the courage to tell him what had happened.

'I had to do it,' I said. 'He killed a person, Ajoba, he killed someone. I had to do it…' I was trying to justify my actions, but I couldn't speak any more as the rest of my words dissolved into tears. Ajoba came over to me and hugged me, gently at first and then tightly.

'I know,' he said. 'And you did the right thing. I know that in your mind you are doubting yourself. Don't do that. Stop doubting yourself. You did the right thing.'

Ajoba had always known what to say to me when I was upset, and that day, too, he made me feel much better. But I was surprised at his reaction. Knowing him and his general outlook, I had expected him to try and persuade me to change my stand. That's when I realized that I was more important to him than his assessment of a situation. That his support for me was unconditional.

Ajoba tried to mediate between me and my father, but to no avail. My father stopped talking to him as well. But he allowed him to continue visiting my grandfather. And from Ajoba I got to know that my grandfather's health had deteriorated further. He was unable to talk and he couldn't even eat food on his own. Someone, usually a caretaker my father had appointed, had to feed him and bathe him. He never recovered from the shock of that night.

I stayed with Ajoba only for a week, but by the time I left, his house had started feeling like home for me. I didn't want to impose on him though, and I also wanted to be alone. So I found accommodation as a paying guest near my office and moved out.

When the time came, I went to the court and gave my testimony again. I considered myself more prepared this time. My training as a lawyer had taught me how cross-examinations worked. But I was not prepared. Definitely not prepared to hear my brother being called 'the accused'. He looked at me as I testified. I felt his gaze, but did not, could not, meet his eyes. I knew that what I was doing was right, but I still didn't want to look at him while doing it. I knew that if I looked at him, I would not be able to speak; my resolve would have been broken. I knew that looking at him would make me start feeling guilty for putting him there. So I avoided him.

I told the court everything that had happened that day, including our meeting with Mohan—'the deceased' as they called him. 'Crime of passion—a sudden fight', the defence argued. The prosecution countered them, saying it was premeditated, cold-blooded murder. 'The accused' had even switched off his cell phone beforehand to prevent it being traced.

As the trial went on, my grandfather suffered a stroke and had to be hospitalized. He had brain haemorrhage and slipped into a coma. Although I heard about all of this from Ajoba, I could not go to the hospital and see him. My father did not permit me to come anywhere close.

We had a fight again when I insisted that I wanted to see my grandfather. He blamed me again, both for my brother's incarceration, and my grandfather's stroke. He shouted and jabbed his finger at my face, and even went to the extent of physically blocking my way when I tried to go into my grandfather's room at the hospital. And he told me that he never wanted to see me. After a few days, I tried to talk to him again, but he refused. He did not shout at me. He did not scream. He was polite in the manner that one is polite to strangers, and refused to give me access to my grandfather.

For him I was truly no longer his daughter. And so I stayed away, until my grandfather died, three months after he entered the coma.

My father allowed me to attend his cremation. It was the last time that he would treat me as family. Rahul was also there—out on bail for the ceremony. He avoided looking at me. So I, too, kept a safe distance from my father and brother, all that was left of my family. But from that safe distance I stared at them. Trying to take in what was possibly one of the last memories that I would have of my family. When I looked at them from afar, I wanted to go and hug them as I used to when I was younger. But I couldn't do that anymore. I had to force myself to stay at my spot. I stood there, staring at them and at the pyre, and before I knew it my grandfather was gone. As that old sensation of numbness returned, I slipped out from the back. I saw Ajoba there, but I realized that this was one cremation after which he could not and would not console me. My grandfather was like a brother to him.

After a few months of job hunting and applying to law firms, I finally got a job. I shifted to Mumbai with relief. It was August 2011.

19

FIVE MONTHS AGO, IN FEBRUARY 2014, THE SESSIONS COURT gave its verdict on Mohan's murder. I was present when the judge read out the judgement, finding my brother guilty. Four days later, the court sentenced him to imprisonment for life.

I had expected this sentence. The police had told me that it was an open-and-shut case. To my great regret, I couldn't help but agree with them. There was too much evidence. The knife was found in Rahul's bag, with his finger prints on it. The blood on it was proved to be that of Mohan, as was the blood on his clothes. And most damning of all were the witnesses.

That is why even the defence had not tried to deny that he had committed the crime. They had pleaded that it was a crime of passion and should be given a lesser sentence. But the judge had not found any substance in their arguments and had found Rahul guilty of murder. The case was thus disposed of with unexpected speed, unlike the trial of Sandhya's murderers which is still going on in court. In that case, the only evidence of guilt was my testimony, since the murder weapon was never found. And I had not seen them actually kill her; I had only seen them fleeing the spot. So the lawyers for the defence kept on questioning the credibility of my testimony and delaying the judgement. Further, the original defence lawyer, the one who had called me 'cheap', was discharged from that case due to a heart ailment. A new lawyer was appointed in his place, but that process itself took more than six months. The new lawyer asked for time to study the case and to consult his clients, so there were further delays. By then, my brother had already become a convict.

Three months ago, I went to visit Rahul in jail. Blood relatives are allowed to meet convicts and my brother graciously agreed to meet me. As I was no longer a witness, the police and the prosecution did not object to me meeting him either. Had I requested a meeting while the trial was pending, they would have stopped me, out of fear that a conversation with him would lead me to change my stand and turn hostile. But now that the trial was over and my job for the prosecution was done, they did not object. Rahul's lawyer had, of course, appealed to the Bombay High Court, but I would no longer have any role to play in court.

The jail is in the suburbs of Pune. The big board outside says, in both Roman and Devnagri scripts, 'Yerwada Central Jail'. I read it again and again as I waited for my turn to meet my brother. Raghav and Mohammed Ali were also in the same jail. They would be wearing civilian clothing as they were still under trial, while my brother, a convict, would be wearing the prison uniform.

There are two entrances to the jail, a small one for visitors and officials on foot, and a big one for police jeeps and cars. The family members waiting their turns to meet inmates were lined up outside the small gate. Once inside this gate, there is a little ground, presumably for the inhabitants of the jail to walk and exercise in. Then, there is a fortification with high walls to make sure that no one escapes. I am a lawyer, but not being a criminal lawyer, I had never seen a jail before. It was just as I had imagined a jail would be, from books and movies.

Another door leads inside the fortification. But once inside, first comes the jail's bureaucracy. Offices on both sides. How many inmates? How many of them convicts? How many under-trials? All this information is written outside the offices in neat, clean handwriting. Even though the handwriting is clear, I read the lists differently: *How many pigs? How many butchered? How many being fed for slaughter?*

Finally, there is a corridor leading to the cells themselves. But it is interrupted by a memorial. *The Poona Pact was signed here,* the plaque next to it says. Gandhiji was imprisoned here, along with many other freedom fighters, in this jail built by the British. And now the location of his cell is a memorial paying tribute to all of them. The Poona Pact is famous—or notorious, depending on your caste—as the agreement signed between Gandhiji and Dr Ambedkar when the former undertook a fast unto death forcing the latter to give up his demand for a separate Dalit electorate. But the Poona Pact is not what first comes to mind now when thinking of Yerwada Jail. Most people associate the jail with Ajmal Kasab, who was the sole survivor of the 26/11 Mumbai terror attacks and was sentenced to death. He was hanged in this jail and buried here too.

Next door, is the Yerwada open prison. Here, there are no fortifications or tall walls to prevent the prisoners from running away. Instead, there are farms and a handloom mill. Some convicts work here and they are paid for their work. They live here as well, in the fields and not in the cells, in small huts. But they are not to step outside the premises. Despite the absence of fortifications, the open prison is so situated that it is not easy to run away. If they try to escape, they are caught and are sent back to the main jail. Reformation of the criminal is the aim of this concept, not only retribution; in theory, they are taught to be productive and leave behind their criminal habits. It is usually the convicts for life who are sent here, based on their good behaviour, after serving seven years in the jail.

My brother has been given a life sentence, so he might be able to move here after seven years. If Raghav and Mohammed Ali's case had reached as speedy a conclusion, they would have also received a life sentence, and by now, have competed seven years in the jail. They might have been in the open prison already. But as of now, all three of them are housed in Yerwada Central Jail. And the jail stinks. It feels like smoke or stale air is being blown in your face and you are choking, gasping for breath. Once you reach here, you become a number. Your name is gone, your identity gone. Only your crime remains and you become prisoner number XXXX. So, I went into this jail and met Prisoner Number 4593.

We, the family members of the inmates, were ushered into a small cubicle. As I waited for him, I looked around nervously at the others who had accompanied me inside. Most of them seemed familiar with the procedure, though some first-timers looked uneasy, like me. One by one, the inmates were brought to meet their respective visitors.

Then he came. And he was completely different. He had the same unruly, curly hair. His hollow, clean-shaven cheeks had become a bit hollower. His long neck was the same as before and his bushy eyebrows had become bushier. But he was different because his personality had changed completely. He was no longer the talkative, cheerful kid I had spent my childhood with, but looked uncomfortable to be around other people.

Rahul came and stood in front of me. There was wire fencing separating the two of us. The jail superintendent reminded all of us that we had only twenty minutes together. We just looked at each other for a minute. But then I guess we realized that we did not have much time to waste. Wasting time is a luxury.

'I am so sorry,' I said softly, trying to prevent the tears from welling up in my eyes.

He looked at me intently. I had thought that my presence there would surprise him. But he didn't seem surprised at all. It was as if he had expected me to come and apologize. I felt as though I was being x-rayed by his eyes.

'You think that what I did was right? It was right of me to kill him?' he asked. I tried not to flinch at the hoarseness of his voice.

'Yes,' I replied, still softly.

'Then why did you give testimony against me?' he asked, his voice rising. 'You could have given testimony in my favour, or just kept shut. Because of you, I lost my alibi.'

'A fake alibi, Rahul. A fake alibi,' I reminded him. 'And even if I had lied, it would have made no difference to the case. There was too much evidence against you. The police had found…'

'It would have made a difference,' he cut me off. 'It would have showed that you care about me.'

'I do care about you, Rahul. That's why I'm here today,' I replied. I wanted to hold his hand, but I couldn't, because of the fencing. I'd have given anything to be able to touch him.

'What you did was right, Rahul. But what I did was right too,' I said after a pause.

'Then why are you sorry?' he asked me, looking directly into my eyes.

'Because you are my brother. And because you're in jail and I'm not,' I replied.

'You're sorry that you have to see me in prison uniform,' he said in a constricted voice. 'And because you are a lawyer. Because you feel guilty that you are a part of a system which cannot give justice to our mother, or to Sandhya, but can give justice to Mohan, a person who does not deserve to get justice, who is…'

'Everyone deserves to get justice,' I interrupted.

'Really? Then why are you sorry?' he asked again. 'Why do you feel guilty about being a part of this rotten system?'

'The system has always been rotten, Rahul. It hasn't become so overnight,' I replied with a sigh. 'Raghav and Mohammed Ali have been under trial for eight years and they are no closer to getting a verdict. That's injustice too. Poor people are jailed for ages for petty crimes. Rape victims are made fun of and humiliated in court. People like our mother never get justice. This has always been the truth. You were perfectly satisfied with the system till our mother got hurt. And now it hurts you so you want to shout "injustice" from the roof tops.'

'But I am shouting now, at least,' he rejoined in a low but firm voice. 'Yes, I shout because I want to be free, out of prison. But I am shouting at last. You never shout, never. You help the system to flourish. You put me in jail by testifying against me and then you say what I did was right. How can both of us be right, Janaki? How?'

'You were right because you got justice for our mother,' I replied. 'And I was right because you have no right to give justice. Mohan had the right, as every criminal does, to be tried and sentenced by the court. You violated that right.'

'But the judiciary violated that right too,' Rahul banged his fist on the table. 'It violated that right by not trying him at all. He was not even arrested for killing our mother and I go to jail for killing him? What justice is this?' His voice was rising with every word.

For a minute I was speechless. I could feel the tears building in my eyes again and I looked away. After a pause I looked at him and replied, 'It is not fair. You should not be in jail. At least, not for life.'

'Then why did you give testimony?' he asked exasperatedly.

'You didn't have the right to get justice for our mother. Similarly, it is not for me to decide what sentence you should get. It's for the courts to decide. I told the truth about what happened to Sandhya and I told the truth about you as well. That's all I can do,' I replied.

'All you can do is to protect and support a system which

doesn't give justice,' he said, his voice rising again. 'Can't you tell a small lie to promote a greater truth? The truth is that Mohan deserved what he got.'

'And who decides if Mohan deserved to die?' I asked. I was feeling very tired all of a sudden, but I pushed myself to continue. 'If we take the law into our own hands, we'll all just be killing each other. Who is going to decide what is just? You?'

'So that is why you want to let the court decide. Let the "honourable judge" decide. Let him use his discretion to give justice to Mohan but deny it to our mother,' he replied bitterly.

'There will be anarchy if we don't do this, Rahul!' I cried out.

'And that will be better,' he replied, with finality in his voice. 'The truth is, there is anarchy now also, just not in the open. Then it will at least be open, in full view. It will at least be called anarchy. You lawyers, instead of calling it by its name, hide anarchy by calling it "arbitrariness". But using these fancy names doesn't change the truth. Do you know what my word for the present situation is? "Disguised anarchy". Not arbitrariness. A state of disguised anarchy is what we have now.'

'There are faults in every system,' I replied. 'I'm not defending the system. But destroying the system won't help. We need to reform it from within.'

'Oho! So you are the noble crusader trying to reform the system. The lawyer who wants to stand up for the truth!' he mocked me.

'Stop it, Rahul,' I said, getting angry for the first time.

'You always liked the truth, right?' he asked, peering at me with mock curiosity. 'You told the truth about what happened to Sandhya. And you told the truth about me. The crusader for the truth. But that doesn't apply to Meena, right?'

'Meena?' I asked, flabbergasted.

'Yes, Meena. You don't remember her?' He was serious again. 'She was that teenage girl who worked in our house when we were children. She used to come and sweep and dust and make our beds. Her mother used to come in the evening and wash the utensils and our clothes. Mother fired them because Sunil Uncle said that she had stolen his money when he came to stay with us. Do you remember her now? She was just a few years older than you …'

'Yes, I … I r-r-remember her. But what does that have to do with what we are talking about now?' I replied, stammering a little.

'Doesn't it? But you said that you speak the truth. So then, why didn't you tell mother that Sunil Uncle was lying? That Meena had not stolen any money? That he had tried to sexually harass her and she had managed to escape him?'

'I was scared. I was a ten-year-old, a kid,' I replied, knowing I sounded defensive.

'I was a kid too,' he interrupted me. 'I was scared too. But I wanted to tell her. We had seen what had happened from our room. Remember how horrified we were? Both of us couldn't sleep that night. But I still wanted to tell… Not only did you not tell, you stopped me as well. You didn't tell the truth that time. You made sure that it remained hidden. What made you a truth lover all of a sudden?

'You are being a hypocrite, Janaki, a hypocrite. You say that I shout from the roof tops now only because it affects me. That's true. But what about you? You told the truth only because what happened affected you. It was only because your best friend was murdered that you withstood pressure and death threats and told the truth. Before that, you were satisfied in turning a deaf ear to the truth. And you and I both know that.'

'I…' I started to speak, but Rahul continued, overriding me.

'And do you want to know why you gave testimony in my case? It was because you want to be able to tell yourself that you are moral. Because you want to be able to tell yourself that you do the right thing, even if it means that your brother has to go to jail. Think once more about why you testified against me. Was it because you wanted the truth to prevail or was it about you?'

I met my brother for twenty minutes. I was hoping to get rid of a burden and my guilt by meeting him. But when the jail superintendent interrupted our conversation mid-sentence, sending Rahul back and me outside, I got up and left without looking back. I was not relieved. As I sat in the bus on my way back to Mumbai, I rang up Ajoba and requested him to come and live with me. He did not question why. I did not tell him about my visit. I don't think I will be seeing Yerwada Central Jail again.

AJOBA

20

SHE HAS REACHED HALF WAY TO PUNE. SHE CALLED ME from the road, where she has stopped to eat vada pao. That's a culinary tradition for most passengers on this route, and Janaki, for one, religiously abides by it. She will be here in about two hours. Or maybe less. The speed and efficiency of cars has improved now. I must not forget that. Then she will take me and the rest of my possessions to Mumbai. Goodbye Pune, it will be.

I grew up in this city and I have watched it grow. When I was young, it was much smaller. It has grown by leaps and bounds and at an unimaginable pace. It's mind boggling for an eighty-five-year-old man like me sometimes. It is a city of migrants like any other, but not the way Mumbai is. It is not the promised land of Mumbai; no one comes here with the aspiration of becoming a millionaire. And yet, the city has grown and has accommodated more and more new people. Some of these new people are professionals. The IT sector is booming. Engineers, software engineers, MBA graduates. They live in new suburbs which have blossomed in the last couple of years. Some of these suburbs are so posh that you will not believe that you are in India. Determined, ambitious professionals. All wanting to make money, have good jobs and great careers.

And then, there is another section of new people, equally determined, trying to get their children and, if possible, themselves, out of poverty. They live in slums—new slums which have also blossomed right next to our posh suburbs, serving as a constant reminder of the inequality in our country, a constant reminder that you are indeed in India.

I don't think that I will see this city again. And quite frankly, I don't want to. This is the city in which, for the last ten years, I have seen people dying. My wife was the first to leave me. She had cancer. Breast cancer. It was diagnosed fifteen years ago when she was sixty-five. It was diagnosed at a very early stage and so it was operated upon. She lost a breast and nothing more to cancer. We were glad. She did not even have to go through chemotherapy at that time. But the operation was a painful task. A tube drained the contaminated blood and fat from her for a month afterwards. She had to take painkillers and antibiotics and then she was fine. Modern medicine saved my wife's life.

Four years later, she was again diagnosed with cancer, this time of the intestine. It was already in the advanced stage. The doctors recommended chemotherapy. My wife lost all her hair. But this time, the loss could not prevent her death. All it could do was to prolong her life. I had thought that this was a good thing in the beginning—this prolonging. By the end, I was not so sure.

I would sit outside the chemotherapy room waiting for her. At the beginning I had made a resolution to be strong and to think positively. I kept telling her that she had got out of it once, and that she would get out of it again. As the days passed, I realized that I was not talking to her at all. I was talking to myself. She listened to me patiently, even in her weak condition, knowing that for the first time in our married life, I was deceiving her. And she accepted the deception. Maybe because she knew that my true intention was to deceive myself. I had decided to be strong, but I could not be strong. She was dying and she had the strength to listen to my lies when she knew that she was dying.

Medical science could not help us this time. It prolonged her life and I was glad to be able to have a few more moments with her. I had spent more than forty years of my life with her. And I cared. I believed in, and even today I believe in, the institution of marriage. I didn't want to let go. So I made myself believe that her suffering was good. Because I did not know what my future would be without her. And she? She suffered and died. The doctors surrendered and raised their hands in defeat.

I had always assumed that I would die before her. So, naturally, I had never given a thought to how I would live without her. In a span of five years, I could have lost her twice. And I did lose her in the end. She was gone and I couldn't do anything. I bowed before nature and accepted its verdict. It had proven, once more, who is the master.

My wife had lived a life when she died. Perhaps not the whole of it, but substantially. She had enjoyed life and suffered its burdens. She had experienced most of the things that life has to offer—both good and bad. But Sandhya hadn't. She had just begun living her life when it was taken away from her, not even by nature, but by the brutality of monsters. She was declared dead on arrival at the hospital. Again, the doctors admitted defeat and we cremated her.

Janaki swallowed that bitter pill too. Her closest friend

was gone. Sandhya's parents lost their only child. There was nothing any of us could do about it. All we could do was to go to court. And we are still stuck there.

Anita experienced life, more so than Sandhya. She also experienced drowning. She was in the ICU for three days. She was bombarded with medications and saline and put on the ventilator. At the end of three days, the doctors gave up again and we went to the crematorium again. But this time, there were no courts.

My friend Shridhar had lived his life almost completely. Ever since Sandhya died eight years ago, he had been dying a little every day. He also saw his daughter-in-law die. His wife had already left him. And his grandson? His grandson had killed. Killed a man—killed a murderer—killed a beast— and killed himself. He had become a number in prison. Yes, Shridhar died finally after living a full life.

Full life? Living life completely? What does it mean? I struggled in my youth. I worked hard. I believed in a better life for myself and my family. I wanted to achieve something, to prove myself. I wanted to help people and influence them. I wanted to 'live my life completely'. I fought for my independence, believed in individual freedom and my worth as a human being. I asserted that I had a right to decide, a right to free choice. A right to determine how to live my life. I built my life and I built my nest, insisting that it would be the way I wanted it to be. My aim, my struggle, every moment of every day, was to live a full life. And at the end of my struggle, I am told that my struggle is futile, for my life has no value. I lived the life that I lived because nature permitted me to and because nobody killed me.

You run on a road to reach a destination. And when you have run for a long time and at the best of your capacity and are about to fall down in exhaustion, you are told, not that you have failed to reach that destination—that would be more bearable—but that there is no destination at all.

It doesn't matter to the person who is murdered that her murderers are in jail. It doesn't matter, because she doesn't exist anymore. She is gone. We can choose our professions, our partners in life. We can make decisions about the events in our life. But our life, our existence, is not our choice. We are alive at this moment and can stop existing the next. And we can fight and suffer till we die. But we will stop existing at some point and from that point onwards it will be as if we never lived. Our struggles and our pains will be futile.

We feel. We associate ourselves with each other. We feel pain. I used to feel pain too. It is great to be able to feel pain. It's a wonderful feeling. Because as long as you feel pain you are under the misconception that your life has value. But now that I don't feel pain, I long for that feeling. My life has no meaning, but I can't die. Because my death has no meaning either. Existence includes both life and death. My existence has no meaning.

But yet I exist and I am conscious and my state of consciousness becomes my tormentor. I live because my life is not my choice. My birth was not my choice and neither will be my death. I don't forcibly try to give my life any meaning. I don't try to make my life my choice. I await the verdict of those whose choice it is. Fate.

But I have my victory, I take my revenge over fate. I accept fate's supremacy. But the meaninglessness of my life makes fate's victory unimportant. I am so insignificant that defeating me is a joke. I laugh at fate because it fights with me. I don't let it boast of its achievements either. I take my revenge.

Janaki will be here in some time. She calls me a cynic. I am glad that she still feels pain.

JANAKI

21

I KNOW THAT AJOBA WILL BE WAITING ANXIOUSLY, SO I called to tell him about my vada pao break and let him know that I would reach Pune in an hour and a half or so. I find his anxiety warming.

I haven't told him yet that I met Rahul. Maybe I'll tell him on our way back. Or maybe I won't tell him at all. He doesn't need to know. When I was young, I used to tell my family members and him a lot about what happened in my life. The things that I wanted to share. Now my family is gone, and I tell Ajoba what he needs to know. He is coming to live with me. We are going to run out of topics of conversation very soon, I'm afraid, far too soon.

But what can I tell him? Can I tell him that it is my fault that Sandhya died? The medical shop was open. I could have asked the men there to help me, to save Sandhya. I got scared. I had asked the waiters at the restaurant, but I didn't have the courage to ask the men at the medical shop. I just froze with fear. I saw them drinking. I didn't want to get raped. I lacked the courage, so I let my friend die. I let her die and I saw her dying. I wasted time. I did nothing to help. I could have called my father earlier. I could have tried to attack the men who were raping her. I could have tried to save her life. But I might have died as well in the process. So I didn't. I let her die. and I escaped without a scratch on my body. My mind was affected, but my body was intact. And it is a body you need to live. Or so I thought.

The reason I testified even after being insulted and threatened was not primarily because I wanted justice for her. It was because I wanted to be able to live with myself. Ever since that day, the image of her being raped is replayed in my head again and again, all the time. But there is always one alteration. And this alteration gives me scope for creativity. Every time, I react in a different way. I do something different and Sandhya is saved. In the eight years that have passed since then, I have imagined a huge number of alternative responses. And the one that comes to mind first is that I could have asked those men at the medical shop for help. I imagine her being saved, her coming back home, going to college, to shops, getting a job, maybe travelling somewhere...

And then I remember that she was not saved. I did not put my life in danger, back then, to save my best friend, so I put my life in danger, later. I testified.

If only I could get another chance to save her. I won't. But unfortunately, I did get a chance to redeem myself, to save myself. And not surprisingly, I lost it too. I was supposed to go with my mother to meet my aunt. And it was I who was supposed to be thrown into the river. I was the one who was supposed to die of pneumonia. But she took the blow for me and I let her. All those years, I had fought with her, I had shouted at her. I had even stopped talking to her properly in the few days before she was attacked. But she died instead of me. She took my death.

So no, I will never again pray to fate to give me the chance to save somebody else. And I will never be able to save myself either. And I haven't got anybody left to sacrifice, have I?

All of them are gone. Sandhya, my mother, my brother, my father, my grandfather and even Ajoba—I have sacrificed them, all, already. Some of them are alive, but they are all gone—all because of me. If only I'd had the courage to ask the men near the medical shop for help. They would have all been available. All of them would have been there. Available for me to sacrifice at some later stage in life.

But it is no surprise that I did not have the courage. I didn't have the courage when I was ten, nor did I have it when I was twenty, and I don't have it now. Rahul was correct. It is about me. It has always been about me.

So I won't ask for any more chances. But unfortunately, fate, it seems, has decided to keep on giving me chances. And I have decided to keep on losing them.

Some day, perhaps, I'll become somebody else's lost chance.

THE LONG MARCH

Namita Waikar

'This sensitive novel explores the fallout of the agrarian crisis, especially in Maharashtra, where a fifth of the 310,000 farmer suicides recorded across twenty years have occurred. A moving and humane tale of that great catastrophe, it reflects damage and despair, but also a hope for change amidst one of the greatest tragedies of our time.' —P. Sainath, author of *Everybody Loves a Good Drought*

In Vidarbha, yet another debt-laden farmer commits suicide. His death leaves his family—especially his twenty-year-old son, Vikram Sonare—devastated and furious. But Vikram's work with the Agricultural Technology Centre and new-found knowledge of social media inspire him to build a network with youth across India and start a silent revolt.

In Mumbai, twenty-six-year-old Mallika Joshi works with an NGO. While on assignment in Vidarbha, she meets farming families neglected by the government and suffering under the weight of increasing debts. Moved by the hardships they've faced, and inspired by Vikram's efforts, she becomes an integral part of the movement.

Together they embark on an epic mission to draw attention to the plight of farmers and other underprivileged sections of society, and finally mobilize millions of people to march into the major cities of India. After the success of the march, the group transforms into a revolutionary political party. But will the existing political forces allow it to succeed?

Urgent and inspiring, *The Long March* is a necessary story for our time.

Format: Paperback   **ISBN: 978-93-88070-77-5**   **Price: Rs 350**

PILGRIMAGE

Ira Singh

'Ira's writing is masterful…very real yet intensely sublime.'—*DNA*

From early to middle age, *Pilgrimage* tells the story of Monica—Mona at home—over three defining, pivotal events in her life.

In the opening section, set in contemporary times, Monica, now a woman with a penchant for causes and sympathy for the dispossessed and the underdog, is stranded on a highway, surrounded and stalled by aggressive kanwariyas marching to the Ganga, even as her father struggles for life in the ambulance they are travelling on.

Then, going back in time, the novel unearths two incidents which made the girl the woman she has become.

'Punishment' finds Mona stepping into adolescence in a small town in north India in the 1980s, becoming aware of her body and its possibilities for the first time, the norms and attitudes which seek to control it, and the ways in which she can subvert them. But when her mother catches Mona spying on a rooftop homosexual encounter, everything changes.

And the in-between story, 'Transgressions', follows Monica as a young scholar of Delhi University in the 1990s—having rejected the demands of home and parents—conducting research on the psychology of drug-addicts, and a doomed, intense love affair with Ajay, a heroin junkie.

Evocative, precise and spare, *Pilgrimage* is an extraordinary exploration of one life negotiating family, sex, love—and the illusion of home. It is also the story of middle-class India and its dysfunctions, its casual bigotry and paralyzing insecurities.

Format: Paperback   **ISBN: 978-93-86702-03-6**   **Price: Rs 299**